DOCTOR·WHO

The Deviant Strain

Collect all the exciting new Doctor Who adventures:

DOCTOR·WHO

The
Deviant Strain

BY JUSTIN RICHARDS

10 9 8

Published in 2005 by BBC Books, an imprint of Ebury Publishing
Ebury Publishing is a division of the Random House Group

The Random House Group Limited Reg. No. 954009
Addresses for companies within the Random House Group can be found at
www.randomhouse.co.uk

A CIP catalogue record for this book is available from the British Library

The Random House Group Limited makes every effort to ensure that the
papers used in our books are made from trees that have been legally sourced
from well-managed and credibly certified forests. Our paper procurement
policy can be found on www.randomhouse.co.uk

Commissioning Editors: Shirley Patton/Stuart Cooper
Creative Director: Justin Richards
Editor: Stephen Cole

Doctor Who is a BBC Wales production for BBC ONE
Executive Producers: Russell T Davies, Julie Gardner and Mal Young
Producer: Phil Collinson

Cover design by Henry Steadman © BBC 2005
Typeset in Albertina by Rocket Editorial, Aylesbury, Bucks
Printed and bound in Great Britain by
Cox & Wyman Ltd, Reading, Berkshire

For Jac & Steve —
fellow travellers

The day he died was the best of Pavel's life.

They had agreed to meet on the cliffs, between the wood and the stone circle. It was bitterly cold and his feet crunched into the frosted snow.

The full moon reflected off the white ground, casting double shadows eerily across the landscape. Behind him, the brittle, leafless trees clawed up towards the cloudless sky. Ahead of him, the icy stones glinted and shone as if studded with stars.

And beside him, holding Pavel's hand, was Valeria. He hardly dared to look at her in case the dream faded. It had to be a dream, didn't it? The two of them, alone, together, at last.

He did look at her. Couldn't stop himself. Lost himself in her wide, beautiful smile. Watched her ice-blonde hair blown back from her perfect smooth-skinned face. Felt himself falling into sky-blue eyes. A dream…

A nightmare.

Her eyes widened, smile twisting into a shout, then a scream.

Darkness wrapped round them both. A sudden glimpse of the shadowy figures shuffling towards them from the wood. Then hands clamped over their mouths – bony, dry hands as if the trees themselves were grabbing at them.

The world turned as the two of them were dragged off their feet, twisted, carried shouting for help. Pavel's hand was snatched away from Valeria's. The last time he saw the girl's terrified face was as she clawed back at him, desperate to make contact again, desperate for help.

A dark, robed figure stepped between them, blotting out his view. A black hood covered the head, face in shadow with the moon behind like a cold halo. The figure turned towards Valeria.

The last thing Pavel saw was the blackness of another figure looming over him.

The last thing he heard was Valeria's scream. Terror and horror and disbelief. As she saw beneath the hood.

The TARDIS froze for an infinitesimal moment, caught between the swirling colours of the vortex. Then it flung itself forwards, sideways and backwards through infinity.

Despite the battering the outside shell of the TARDIS was taking, inside was quiet and calm. The central column of the main console was doing what it was supposed to do; all the right lights were flashing;

Captain Jack Harkness was whistling and all was well. Jack paused mid-whistle to press a button that really didn't need pressing, then resumed his rather florid rendition of 'Pack up Your Troubles…'

The warning bleep was so perfectly in time with the beat that he didn't even notice it until he was halfway through the next chorus.

'Smile, smile, smile…'

Bleep, bleep, bleep.

Then he was all action. At the console, checking the scanner and scrolling down the mass of information. Not a lot of it made sense, but he nodded knowingly just in case the Doctor or Rose came in.

'A warning?' He checked another readout. 'Cry for help…' Grinned. 'Damsel in distress, maybe.' Probably best not to touch anything. Probably best to wait for the Doctor.

Then again: 'What the hell…'

The Doctor arrived at a run, Rose in his wake. He was stern, she was grinning.

'What's the fuss?' Rose asked.

'Just a distress call,' Jack told her, moving aside as the Doctor's elbow connected with his stomach. 'Nothing much. Happens all the time on the high frontier.'

'Not like this,' the Doctor told him, not looking up from the scanner. 'This is serious stuff.'

As if in reply, the bleeping changed from a regular pulse to a violent cacophony. 'That shouldn't happen.' Slowly, the Doctor turned towards Jack. 'You haven't done anything stupid, have you?'

'What, me? You think I don't know the standard operating procedure?'

'There isn't a standard operating procedure,' Rose reminded him. She was at the console too now, straining to see the scanner. 'Here, let's have a butcher's.'

'Oh, great. Distress call comes in and you want to open a meat shop.'

'Shut it, you two,' the Doctor ordered. 'Someone's responded to the signal, so that's all right.'

'Is it?' Rose asked.

'Yeah. Whoever it was will go and help. Sorted.'

'They will?' Jack asked quietly.

'Bound to. Morally obliged. They get first dibs. No one else'll bother now there's been a response, will they? Automated systems broadcast for help, someone responds and they start streaming all sorts of location data and details. Signal strength's gone up 500 per cent, probably using the last of their back-up emergency power. Though after so long it'll be a waste of someone's time, I expect.'

'I wonder who responded,' Rose said. She was already turning away, dismissing the problem from her mind.

'Er, well,' Jack said. 'Actually…'

The Doctor's mouth dropped open. 'You didn't…' He turned away as Jack started whistling again. 'You did.' He was back at the scanner. 'They're getting pretty frantic now, thinking they're about to be rescued from whatever godforsaken lump of rock they're stuck on. Well, they needn't think I'm going to…' His voice tailed off into a frown.

'Morally obliged,' Jack said quietly.

'Yeah, we should go and help, Doctor,' Rose put in. 'Where are they?'

'Some barren wilderness that's good for nothing,' Jack suggested.

The Doctor looked up, smiling again now. 'It's Earth – early twenty-first century.'

Jack nodded glumly. 'Told you so.'

One of General Grodny's large hands was wrapped around a cut-glass tumbler. His other hand held the remote control for the wall screen. His face was set in a granite grimace that gave no clue as to how much the vodka was burning his throat. But when he spoke it sounded as if his voice was being strained through broken glass – hoarse and discordant and rough.

'How long ago?'

The men with him did not need to ask what he meant. The energy pattern was flashing on the image that covered the screen. They had started with a map of the whole of northern Russia. The energy pulse was a pinprick of yellow on the red background. Then they zoomed in to the Novrosk Peninsula. Then Novrosk itself. Finally this – a satellite picture. It was so clear you could see the base and the old barracks and military facilities. The submarines were dark slugs edging into the frozen water of the bay. The energy pulse was a ripple of discordant colour across the cliff tops.

'It started eleven minutes ago. There may have been some background energy before that, but within

11

tolerance. Nothing to worry about.'

'And why is it not coming from the submarine pens?' the general demanded. 'If it is radiation from the old reactors?' A new thought struck him and he gulped at the vodka. 'Have the missiles been removed?'

'Er, most of them. But there are still some SSN-19s on one of the boats.' The aide swallowed. 'Perhaps several. Actually we don't know.'

Grodny sighed. 'Of course we don't know. We don't know anything. Not any more. Why should we care if there's a radiation leak in the middle of nowhere and a few Shipwreck class Cruise missiles ready to soak it up. You know how many Shipwrecks an Oscar II carries?'

His two aides exchanged glances. They knew. 'With respect, General...'

He answered his own question. 'Twenty-four.'

'This is not a radiation leak, sir.'

'And you know how powerful each of those missiles is?'

'They have been decommissioned, though not removed,' the second aide said nervously. He knew the answer to this question too. 'The warheads have been disabled, but the missiles remain in place.'

'It's not a radiation leak, sir,' the first aide repeated. He was sensible enough not to raise his voice.

'The equivalent of half a million tons of TNT. Twenty-four missiles per boat, perhaps a dozen boats...'

'Fifteen,' the second aide murmured. He was sweating.

'We must be thankful that whatever is leaking does

not set off Cruise missiles.' He swirled the glass, letting the liquid lap round the top. 'Even if it will kill everyone on the peninsula.' He sipped again at the vodka. 'As if we hadn't condemned them all to death when we left them there twenty years ago.'

'It's not –'

'I heard you the first time,' the general snarled. 'But if it isn't radiation, what is it?'

No answer.

'Then we need to find out. And we need to tell the Americans that we have a reactor leak that we can handle, in case they get any ideas. Assure them it is not a launch signature.'

The second aide shifted uncomfortably, loosened his stiff collar with a sweaty finger. 'Need we tell the Americans anything, sir? I mean, Novrosk is an ultra-secret establishment – the submarine pens, the scientific base…'

Grodny jabbed a stubby finger towards the screen. 'If we can see it, so can they. If we have tried to keep it secret, you can be sure they have known about it for years. Where is Colonel Levin?'

It took them a moment to realise he had changed the subject. Then the first aide replied, 'His team is on their way back from… that business in Chechnya.'

Grodny nodded, his expression changing for the first time as the trace of a smile was etched on it. 'Send him in.'

'You want to see him, General?'

'No, not here, you fool.' Again he jabbed at the screen.

'Send him in *there*. To find out what's going on.'

'He is expecting to come home, sir,' the first aide ventured. He swallowed. 'I wouldn't like to be the one to tell him…'

'Then order someone else to tell him,' Grodny snapped. 'I want Levin to handle it. He is the best we have. And he'll be in no mood to mess about.' He shifted in his chair, turning to look at the two aides standing nervously beside him. 'Any more than I am.'

Less than ten minutes later, an MI-26 Halo helicopter swung in an arc over Irkutsk and started on a new bearing. A week earlier it had carried a full complement of eighty-five combat troops on its outward journey. Now it was bringing thirty-seven back.

As he slammed down the radio, Colonel Oleg Levin's face was a mask of angry determination.

'It's fading. Power's running down, I s'pose,' the Doctor said. He tapped at the flickering lights on the scanner that represented the pulse beat of the signal.

'They must be in a bad way,' Jack said.

'Do we know who they are?' Rose wondered. The lights and readings meant nothing to her. 'What they are?'

'Probably long dead,' the Doctor decided. 'But since our associate here told them we'd come and help, we'd better check to be sure.'

Jack raised an eyebrow. 'Well, if you don't want to.'

'It's not whether I want to, is it? I'm morally obliged.'

The Doctor nudged him aside as he moved round the console. '*You* morally obliged me.'

'Me too,' Rose reminded them.

'It's a repeating pattern,' Jack told them. 'A loop.'

'Yeah, well, it would be. Like "Mayday, mayday, mayday."'

'Or "SOS, SOS, SOS",' Rose added.

Jack sniffed. 'I just meant maybe we can decipher it. Work out what it means.'

'It means "Help."' The bell at the side of the console dinged and the Doctor thumped at a control. 'Coming?'

Jack was still examining the line of pulse beats on the scanner. 'If it is a loop, maybe we should look at it as a loop.' He flicked at a control and the repeated line bent round on itself to form a circle. The pulses were shown as illuminated patches, slightly different shapes and sizes spaced slightly irregularly.

Rose peered over Jack's shoulder. 'Looks like a map of Stonehenge,' she said. 'Come on, we're getting left behind. As usual.'

'What were you saying about Stonehenge?' the Doctor called as they stepped out of the TARDIS.

'Oh, nothing,' Rose said.

She was glad of her coat, pulling it tight around her against the bitter chill. The bright sunlight seemed to make no impact on the inches of snow lying underfoot.

'That's good. Because…'

The Doctor was striding out across the snow-covered plain, staring at the landscape ahead of them and leaving a trail of footsteps in his wake.

The TARDIS was on the top of a cliff, wind blowing round it, sending Rose's hair into a frenzy and kicking up puffs of snow at her feet. She could hear the crash of the waves from far below. But her attention was on the Doctor. He turned and looked back, grinning.

'Interesting, don't you think?'

To one side of him was a wood, the trees spiky and bare, dripping with icicles. To the other side of the Doctor, on the horizon, stood a line of stones. Standing stones. They seemed to glitter in the cold sunlight, as if studded with quartz that was catching the light.

'A stone circle,' Rose said. 'That's a coincidence.'

'Coincidence, my –'

But Jack's words were drowned out by the sudden roar of sound. The wind was blowing up even more. Snow blasting across the cliff and stinging Rose's eyes.

A huge helicopter, like a giant metal spider, was hanging menacingly in the air, level with the top of the cliff. A door slid open halfway along its side, and a man leaped out – a soldier. Khaki uniform, heavy pack, combat helmet, assault rifle. And behind him a line of identical figures leaping to the ground, keeping low, spreading out in a circle and running to their positions.

The Doctor wandered slowly back to join Rose and Jack. 'Welcoming party?' he wondered.

The circle complete, the soldiers levelled their rifles – aiming directly at the Doctor and his friends. The first man out of the helicopter was walking slowly towards the middle of the circle. His own rifle was slung over his shoulder and he moved with confidence and determination. He stopped directly in front of the Doctor.

And, just from his eyes, Rose could tell he was furious.

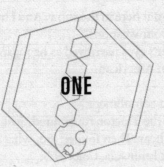

ONE

'What are you doing here, near the village?' the soldier snapped. 'If they call it the village.'

'What would you call it?' the Doctor asked.

'Community,' the soldier suggested. He was a large man – broad and tall, bulked out by his combat uniform and heavy pack. 'Dockyard. Institution.'

'You make it sound like the madhouse,' Rose said.

The soldier swung round to look at her properly. 'I'd be surprised if they aren't all mad by now. Twenty years abandoned and forgotten out here. Even with the base.'

'They?'

'I'm sorry?'

'You said "they",' the Doctor replied. 'As if you think we're not from this community dockyard institution village. Whatever we settle on calling it.'

'You're not dressed for this climate,' the soldier said.

'Neither are you,' Jack pointed out. 'You aren't equipped for near-Arctic warfare, are you? Khaki is no camouflage out here in the snow. And I bet you haven't winterised your weapons.'

The soldier's eyes narrowed as he regarded Jack. 'You speak like an American.'

'Thanks.'

'It wasn't a compliment.'

'Russian,' the Doctor murmured, just loud enough for Rose to hear. Then louder: 'So, what brings you to the Novrosk Peninsula, Colonel?'

'I have my orders.'

'Yeah, well, we've got ours too. You think you've been yanked out here at short notice, you should see what happened to us.'

Rose could see the soldier tense slightly as the Doctor reached inside his jacket. He kept the movement slow and careful, grinning to show he meant no harm. When he withdrew his hand, Rose could see that he was holding a small leather wallet. He opened it out to reveal a blank sheet of paper. Psychic paper – it would show the person looking at it whatever the Doctor wanted them to see.

'Like I said, we've got our orders.'

The soldier nodded slowly, reading the blank page. 'I hope you don't expect me to salute, Doctor... I'm sorry, your thumb is over your name.'

'Yeah.' The Doctor stuffed the wallet back inside his jacket. 'Right, this is Rose Tyler, my number two. And Captain Jack Harkness here is from Intelligence.'

Jack was grinning too. 'You don't need to know which branch. I'm sure you can make a very good guess.'

The Doctor clapped his hands together. 'So, we're all mates, then, eh?' His smile faded. 'And no – there's no need to salute. Just so long as you do what I need you to do, then we won't get in your way. Fair enough?'

'So, who are you, then?' Rose wanted to know.

The soldier had turned and was gesturing to his men. The rifles snapped up, and the soldiers turned and started to move slowly and carefully across the cliff top. Some were heading for the stone circle, others towards the wood.

'It seems you have been as well briefed as we have,' the soldier said as he turned back. 'I am Colonel Oleg Levin. Like you, we are here to investigate the energy spike the satellite picked up. Like you, I would rather not be here. So perhaps we can make this as quick and easy and straightforward as possible.'

'Right,' the Doctor agreed.

'Despite what they are telling us, I assume the energy was released from one of the submarines, or from the scientific base.'

'That's what we think,' Jack agreed.

'What submarines?' Rose said.

'What scientific base?' the Doctor wondered.

Levin looked at each of them in turn. 'You haven't been briefed at all,' he realised. 'Typical. I'm surprised you even know where you are.' He sighed and made to move away. As he did so, he seemed to notice the TARDIS for the first time.

'Oh, that's ours,' Rose said.

'Equipment,' the Doctor explained. 'Stuff. We just got

dumped here, like you.'

Levin nodded. 'Shambles,' he muttered. 'You have Geiger counters?'

'Think we'll need them?' the Doctor asked.

Levin laughed. 'Don't you?'

He turned back towards his men, now disappearing over the snowy horizon. The Doctor, Jack and Rose exchanged looks. The Doctor was shaking his head. 'No radiation readings much above background,' he said quietly.

'You did check, then?' Rose said. She was shivering now, the cold biting into her bones.

'Oh yeah. I think.'

'Think?!'

A snarl of anger and frustration interrupted them. Levin had a hand to his ear, reaching under his helmet, and Rose guessed he was wearing a radio earpiece. He turned back to them, addressing the Doctor: 'I'm sorry, sir...'

'Just Doctor.'

'Doctor. I think we may have a problem.'

'Define problem,' Jack snapped.

'A body. In the stone circle.'

Both Rose and Jack were shivering, though Jack was trying not to show it. The Doctor sent them back to the TARDIS to get warmer coats while he went with Colonel Levin to see the body.

'Have you seen much death?' the colonel asked as they walked across the snowy ground.

'Why d'you ask? Think I'm a wimp?'

'No. But this body is… interesting.'

'Is that what they tell you?'

'Well?'

'I'm a Doctor.'

'You could be a doctor of philosophy.'

He grinned. 'That too.'

Colonel Levin stopped. The Doctor stopped as well, sensing that this was the moment when he needed to win the man over. 'Yeah?'

'I resent being here,' Levin said levelly. 'I resent *you* being here. You interfere, you slow me down, and I don't care what your notional rank might be or who your intelligence officer really is. I have a job to do and I'm going to do it. So cut the wise cracks and the inane grin. If you're good at what you do, prove it and we'll get along fine. If you're not, then keep out of the way and you might survive with your career intact. Clear?'

'As the driven snow.'

'Good.'

Levin turned and strode off. It took him several paces before he realised the Doctor was not following. Slowly, reluctantly, he turned and walked back.

'I know how you feel,' the Doctor said. 'I didn't ask to come here. But now I'm here, I've got a job to do as well. Am I good at what I do? I'm the best. That's why I do it. Rose and Jack, they're the best too – so you don't give them any hassle, right?' He didn't wait for a reply. 'You want to know if I've seen much death? I've seen more than you can ever imagine. So cut the tough-guy bit and prove to me that you're good at what you do. Clear?'

'As the driven snow,' Levin said quietly. 'Sir.'

The grin was back. The Doctor clapped his hand to Levin's shoulder, encouraging him forwards. 'I told you, it's not "sir" it's just "Doctor". Hey,' he went on, 'they tell me *you're* the best. You and your men. So we should get on famously. Let's do the job and get home for tea.'

Though the Doctor had insisted he was not actually a doctor of medicine, Levin was impressed with the man's analysis of the body.

It was lying beside one of the standing stones on the far side of the circle – the side closest to the village. Looking down into the valley, Levin could see the dilapidated huts and the abandoned dockyards lining the inlet. The stumpy black shapes of the submarines in their rusting pens. It was hardly picturesque, but it was preferable to looking at the body. The man who'd found it had coughed his guts up a few paces away. At least he'd had the sense not to disturb the evidence – if it was evidence. Ilya Sergeyev – hero of Borodinov, a soldier who'd killed a dozen men at close range in the last week with his gun, his knife and even his bare hands – puking up at the sight of a body.

But then Levin had tasted bile and turned away when he'd seen it too. The Doctor, for once, had looked serious and grim as he knelt to examine it.

'Cause of death, hard to say,' the Doctor decided.

'Need more to examine really. I mean, it's all here. Recent from the state of the clothes, but the corpse has all but wasted away. I guess the clothes fitted before…'

He raised a sleeve of the heavy coat. A frail, withered hand emerged from the end of it. Flopped back down.

'I mean, feel the weight of that. Bones are completely atrophied. As if they've been sucked out or dissolved. Gone.' He sighed and got to his feet. 'Jellified. Don't let Rose see it.'

Levin nodded. He could see the girl and the young man at the other edge of the circle and nodded to Lieutenant Krylek to go and intercept them. 'Then send someone down to the village. Find the Barinska woman and get her up here to see this.'

'Who's she? Why inflict it on her?' the Doctor wondered.

'She's the police officer. The only police officer. This is her problem, not mine.'

'No,' the Doctor told him. 'It's everyone's problem.' He dusted his hands together, as if to show he had finished with the body, and wandered across to the nearest stone.

Levin followed him, and a moment later Rose and Jack joined them.

'Interesting composition.' The Doctor ran his hands over the stone.

'Twenty-four of them,' Jack said. 'Not quite evenly spaced. A repeating pattern,' he added with emphasis, though Levin couldn't see why that might be significant.

'I like the way they sparkle,' Rose said. 'Is that quartz or something doing that?'

'Possibly.' The Doctor was rubbing at the stone. 'It's as if they're polished. Shiny. No weathering.'

'Are they new?' Jack wondered.

'They were here twenty years ago,' Levin told them. 'They looked as new and felt as smooth then as they do now.'

'How do you know?'

'Because I was here. When it all ended. Or maybe when it began, at least for the poor souls they left behind. For Barinska and the others.'

'Tell us about it,' the Doctor said.

'Didn't they brief you *at all*?'

'Let's assume not.'

So Levin told them.

'It was one of my first assignments after training. The Cold War was coming to an end, Russia was disarming. We couldn't afford to keep the same level of military spending. There were two installations here at Novrosk.' He pointed across at the squat, squared-off buildings round the harbour. 'The dockyards and barracks.' Then in the other direction, towards a low-lying concrete complex. 'The research station.'

'Research?' Jack asked.

'Secret, of course. Everything here is – was – secret. The submarine base and the Organic Weapons Research Institute.'

'Organic?' Rose's nose wrinkled. 'I take it that isn't like organic vegetables.'

'That's what you're left with after deployment, probably,' Jack said.

The Doctor waved them both to silence. 'Let him finish, can't you?'

'They kept the research institute open,' Levin explained. 'There are only a few scientists still there, but at least they have funding, they get supplies and they appear on some paperwork. They exist.'

'And the docks?' the Doctor prompted.

Two tiny figures in khaki were just visible jogging down the snowy hill, reaching the edge of the concreted track leading into the dock area. It was as if the snow didn't dare settle on the old military base.

'They closed it down. Left the submarines to rot. We were supposed to decommission them. Rip out whatever was of use and take it away. Same with the community – we took the sailors and the troops and the higher-grade workers. Left the rest. To rot.'

'You mean, people?' Rose said.

'I mean people. There was a whole civilian infrastructure built up round the base. Mechanics and caterers, fishermen and farmers. They relied on the docks and the military for their livelihood.'

'So the military pulled out and left them… Left them what?' the Doctor asked.

Levin shrugged. 'Just left them. I don't imagine they'll be grateful for our return.' In the distance, a cluster of tiny dark shapes – people – were gathered round the two soldiers at the edge of the docks.

'And the submarines?' Jack asked. 'You said they were

supposed to be stripped and decommissioned, right? Only, you mentioned radiation.'

Levin nodded. The guy wasn't daft after all. Working in Intelligence was no guarantee of a share of it, but he could obviously think. 'It's expensive to completely close down nuclear reactors. We've "decommissioned" about 150 subs in the last ten years. Not a single one has yet had its reactor removed.'

'Oh, great.' Rose blew out a long, misty breath. 'You're telling us there's any number of submarines down there with dodgy nuclear reactors.'

Levin smiled thinly. 'Fifteen.' He waited for them to absorb this before adding, 'And there are the missiles too, of course.'

Sofia Barinska was, as Levin had said, the only figure of recognised authority in the community. She was also one of the few with transport. Her battered four-wheel drive screeched to a protesting halt beside the stones. The door creaked as she pushed it open. She glared at Levin and his men, frowned at the Doctor and his friends, shook her head as she caught sight of the blanket covering the body.

'You're lucky I have any fuel left,' she told Levin. 'Don't expect a lift.'

'I'm surprised you have any fuel at all. You get it from the institute?'

She snorted. 'Where else? Who else knows we are here?'

Rose was watching Levin, surprised at how he was

frowning at the woman, as if there was something wrong. But she looked normal enough to Rose – despite being wrapped in a thick coat, her jeans tucked into heavy walking boots, the woman was obviously fit and attractive. Her face was weathered and she looked tired, but Rose guessed she was in her thirties. Her dark hair was tied back in a bun that made her look severe and official.

Barinska had noticed Levin's stare as well. She glared back. 'What is it, Colonel? You're going to reprimand me for not wearing my uniform, is that it? If so, you should know it fell apart years ago.'

'I'm sorry. I thought… I thought I recognised you.'

She was surprised. 'You have been here before?'

'For the decommissioning.'

'Ah. But that was twenty years ago. Perhaps you remember my mother.'

'Keeping it in the family?' Rose asked.

The policewoman turned and glared hard at her. 'This is a closed community. No one comes, no one can leave. What else would we do?'

Rose looked away. 'Sorry. Er, where's your mum now?'

'In the ground.' Without any apparent emotion or further thought on the matter, she nodded at the body. 'Show me.'

A glimpse was enough, then Rose turned away. Jack joined her. A minute later, the Doctor wandered over.

'Don't worry about it,' he told Rose. 'They're all hurting a bit. They've been hurting for years. And now this…'

'Does she know who it is?' Rose wondered.

'From the clothes, she thinks it's a kid who went missing last night. Boy called Pavel Vahlen. His parents thought he'd sneaked out to meet a girl. He never came back.'

'And the girl?' Rose asked.

'Is missing too, yeah. She's just nineteen.' He didn't need to add, 'Like you.'

Two of the soldiers were loading the body into the back of Barinska's vehicle. It was like a cross between a Range Rover and an estate car. Rose could just make out a faded police symbol on the tailgate as it caught the light when they opened it. Like the buildings round the docks below them in the valley, it looked old and worn out.

Levin was giving orders to the soldiers and they began to spread out, moving slowly across the cliff top.

'Where are they going?' Rose wondered.

'Search party.'

'We should help,' Jack said. 'Damsel in distress.'

'Damsel probably dead,' Levin said, joining them.

'Even so,' the Doctor said. 'You could do with some help. How many men have you got?'

'Now?' Levin asked for no apparent reason, though Rose could hear in his voice that it meant something important to him. 'Thirty-six, plus me.'

'Thirty-seven, then,' the Doctor said. 'Plus us. So that's forty.'

Levin nodded. 'You really a captain?' he asked Jack.

'Oh, yes. Born and bred.'

'Then go with Sergeyev and his group – they're checking the woods. Doctor, you and Miss Tyler can go with Lieutenant Krylek – he's heading towards the institute. I'll talk to Barinska. We need the locals on our side.'

'Point out to her,' the Doctor said quietly, 'that they might need you.'

Levin nodded. Then he saluted and left them.

'Right, woods it is,' Jack said. 'See you later, team.' He set off at a jog to catch up with the soldiers.

The snow faded and thinned at the edge of the woods. The ground was visible in patches, more and more of it the further in Jack looked, making the woods seem even darker than they were. The trees were skeletal, stripped bare of leaves and greenery. Like the rusting derricks he had glimpsed down at the docks.

Sergeyev had acknowledged Jack's arrival with a hard stare. Jack hadn't bothered telling the soldier he outranked him. Probably it would make no difference. Probably they would find nothing. The dozen soldiers had fanned out into a line, walking slowly and purposefully through the gloom, rifles held ready across their bodies, angled at the ground. For now.

They were well trained, he could see that. The way they moved – always alert, not hurrying, no sign of impatience, frequently checking on the man either side as they moved onwards.

Boring. It would take for ever like this. Jack had no idea how big the wood was, but he didn't fancy being stuck in it for hours. As the Doctor said, the girl was probably dead anyway. Jellified like the poor teenager up at the circle.

Teenager? He'd looked about ninety.

So Jack found himself moving ahead of the soldiers. He earned sighs and glares as he advanced past them. He smiled and waved to show he didn't care, and he carried on at his own pace.

She was lying so still, he almost tripped over her.

Face down, her arms extended, gloved hands gripping the base of a tree as if holding on for dear life. But there was no grip in her fingers as he gently eased them away. Jack thought she was dead, but in the quiet of the wood he could hear her sigh, could see the faint trace of warm breath in the cold air.

'Over here!' he yelled to the soldiers.

They were there in seconds. Several stood with their backs to Jack and the others, watching behind them, alert to the possibility of ambush. Sergeyev stooped down beside Jack. He looked about twenty at most, Jack thought, as the slices of sunlight that got through the trees cut across the soldier's face. Just a kid, really.

'She's breathing,' Jack said. He rolled the girl over on to her back. Her hair was so fair it was almost white, spread across, hiding her face. He brushed it gently away with his fingers.

Sergeyev was speaking quietly into his lapel mike. His words froze as the girl's face appeared from under the strands of hair.

She was nineteen, the Doctor had said. From the

shape of her body, from the hair and the clothing, from the startlingly blue eyes that were staring up at him, Jack could believe it. But her face was lined and wrinkled, dry and weathered. Jack was staring at the face of an old woman.

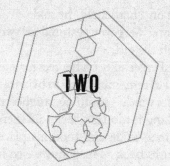

TWO

He could see how she had been, how she must have looked, before whatever had happened to her.

'It's all right, we're here to help.'

But how would she cope – did she even know how she looked now?

No response. Nothing. She didn't even blink. Jack could see she was breathing – the movement of her chest, the mist from her immobile lips. But the blue eyes were glazed and fixated, no expression on her lined face. Nothing. He waved his hand in front of her eyes. Again, nothing.

Sergeyev caught Jack's hand with his own. The soldier was shaking his head. 'She's gone,' he said. 'I have seen it on the battlefield. Shock, trauma. You just leave them to die.'

Jack pulled his hand away. He levered the girl upright into a sitting position. She didn't resist, but she did nothing at all to help. Still there was no acknowledgement that they were even there.

'We're not on a battlefield,' he said.

'Are you sure?' Sergeyev gestured for two of the other soldiers to lift the girl.

She swayed unsteadily on her feet for a few moments, then seemed to remember how to balance. The soldiers walked her forwards – shuffling, stubborn steps at first.

'You're taking it too fast,' Jack told them. He moved one of the men aside and took his place, arms tight round the girl's back as he gently eased her forwards. 'Come on, you can do it,' he murmured.

There was no sign she could hear. What the hell had happened to her? He had her full weight now, and the other soldier shrugged away and looked to Sergeyev, who nodded.

'Let's get her back to the stone circle,' Jack said.

'They are already waiting,' Sergeyev told him.

To Sofia Barinska's undisguised annoyance, Levin had commandeered her car. One of the soldiers was sitting in the driving seat, and Sofia was leaning against one of the stones, glaring and smoking a thin cigarette.

Sergeyev's message came before they drove the body away. The Doctor and Rose arrived with the other troops before Jack and Sergeyev's contingent.

'We were going to take the body over to the research institute,' Levin told the Doctor. 'I'd rather the medical officer there took a look at him than some quack from the village.'

'You don't think they have a decent doctor in the village?' Rose asked.

'If they had, he'd have left long ago,' Levin said.

He glanced at Sofia as he spoke, and Rose wondered what he had deduced about her competence. She had grown up here, Rose supposed – what training had she had, if any?

One of the soldiers called across, pointing towards the woods. Rose could see the other troops returning now, leaving a dark trail behind them in the snow. In the middle of the group, Rose could see Jack. He was all but carrying a young woman, pulling her along beside him. As they got closer, Rose could see that he was talking to her, encouraging her every step of the way, as if she was a small child who'd just learned to walk.

Except that when they got closer still Rose could see that the girl had the face of an old woman. She stumbled, almost fell – dragging Jack with her. He regained his balance with difficulty and pulled her along again.

'Well, help him,' Rose called out. Were they worried she might be infectious or something?

Two of the soldiers with Levin ran to help. But Jack snarled something at them and they stepped aside. Well, that answered that one. Rose ran over, the Doctor beside her.

'Don't be so proud,' she hissed at Jack. 'You're exhausted.'

He pushed her away with his free hand. But the Doctor eased him aside and took the girl's weight. 'I know,' he said gently. 'She has to do this on her own. Or as much as she can. It's OK. Really, it's OK.' He might have said this to Jack or to the girl.

Grudgingly, Jack allowed the Doctor to take over. But he stayed beside the girl, and asked, 'What's her name? Who is she?'

It was Sofia Barinska who answered. She pushed herself off the stone she had been leaning on and flicked away the stub end of her cigarette. 'Her name is Valeria Mamentova.' The policewoman crossed herself quickly and muttered something.

'What happened to her?' Rose wondered.

The Doctor and Jack leaned Valeria against the stone where Sofia had been. Jack was breathing heavily.

'Same as happened to the boy, Pavel, I'd say. Only a less extreme dose,' the Doctor guessed.

'What could do this?' Jack asked.

By way of reply, the Doctor turned towards Sofia. 'What do you think?'

She shrugged. 'Some disease or infection.'

'Yeah, right.' The Doctor nodded. 'And what do you *really* think?'

The woman turned and held his gaze. 'Vourdulak,' she said. Then she gave a snort of anger and waved her hand dismissively. 'What do I know?'

'You'll come with us to the institute,' Levin told her.

'If I must.'

'I can't make you,' he said. 'But I am asking.'

'Very well. But I shall drive.'

She walked over to the car and opened the driver's door. After a moment, the soldier sitting there got out.

'Let's get her into the car,' the Doctor told Jack.

'Maybe they can help at this science base.'

'Or not.'

'So what did she mean by Vourdulak?' Rose said. 'Or is it just me who's confused here?'

'The Vourdulak is a creature from Russian folklore,' the Doctor explained. 'It's a vampire that takes the form of a beautiful young woman, though it's really an ancient and evil monster.'

Rose held open the back door of the car as Jack helped the girl inside. Valeria's wrinkled face still showed no expression, her eyes still stared sightlessly ahead.

'So, what? She reckons the poor girl was got by this vampire thing?'

Jack didn't reply. He climbed into the back beside Valeria.

'Am I missing something here?' Rose demanded.

The Doctor led her a few steps away from the car. 'Or it could be she thinks the poor girl *is* the vampire thing.'

There was a medical unit at the base, but no doctor.

'There's only the four of us now,' the Head of Projects explained. 'We're lucky if we can get sticking plaster, never mind staff.'

His name was Igor Klebanov and he was a short, dark-haired man who, despite his protestations about the lack of comforts, was tending towards stout.

All four of the staff were gathered in the small medical unit, evidently excited to have company. A tall man with thinning grey-streaked hair introduced himself as Alex Minin. 'I'm not a scientist,' he apologised. 'I stayed on to handle the admin side of things.'

'Not being a scientist, they didn't transfer poor Alex,' Klebanov put in. 'And Boris and Catherine are only here for two years as part of their university training.'

'Monkeying about,' Boris Brodsky said. He grinned as if it was a joke, and Rose saw that Alex Minin glared back at him, as if he was on the receiving end of it. Boris coughed and added, 'Two years is more than enough.' He was in his mid-twenties, with red hair and freckles, and he seemed unable to stop grinning. 'I shan't be upset to leave. I don't know why *you* stayed.' This was to Klebanov, but again Rose felt there was a dig at Minin.

'I don't like to leave things unfinished. I was here during the Cold War years,' Klebanov explained to the newcomers. 'I was chief scientist when the base was all but closed down.'

'You must have been very young,' the Doctor said.

'Perhaps I am older than you think?'

'P'raps we all are,' the Doctor joked.

Bored with the male banter, Rose stepped aside to chat to the only woman on the base. Catherine Kornilova told her that she was a mature student, studying for a higher degree in nuclear physics.

'So you're quite at home here with the submarines and stuff,' Rose guessed.

The woman smiled thinly. 'Quite the opposite. I know how dangerous it is. Like Boris, I can't wait to leave. I just hope I can find another job. Otherwise I'll be stuck here like poor Alex.'

'Can't he just transfer somewhere else?'

'Maybe.' She shrugged. 'He was the political officer here. With that on his record, it's difficult. But I sometimes think it's even harder for him to stay.'

'Why?'

'Because everyone who was here back then – everyone except me and Boris, I suppose – they remember who he was and what he did. How he watched and reported everything. And they hate him for it. Even Klebanov. Even Boris, I think.'

Rose looked across at Alex Minin, and found that he was looking back at her. For a moment their eyes met, then the tall man looked away, running his hand through his thinning hair to make it seem as if he wasn't watching them at all.

'Right, then,' the Doctor announced, clapping his hands together. 'Everyone out. I need a bit of peace and quiet to examine the patient and the body.'

That jolted Rose. Talking to Catherine, she had almost forgotten there was a dead body under a sheet on the other side of the room. And a young woman whose mind had been emptied and her body aged, sitting silent and helpless beside the corpse.

Levin gestured for the few of his men who were with them to leave. Most he had already sent to patrol the village or guard the base, though against what threat no one asked. Others were helping themselves to equipment from the base stores.

Sergeyev paused on his way out. He looked over at

Jack, standing beside Valeria. 'I guess the captain likes older women,' he said to the soldier beside him. They both laughed and turned to go.

But Jack was across the room in a moment, grabbing Sergeyev's shoulder and turning him round. His eyes were blazing angry.

'Sir?' Sergeyev said. 'I assume I call you "sir", even though you are in Intelligence.'

The mockery in his voice was plain, and the room was suddenly silent around them. Rose swallowed, hoping Jack would let it go, but knowing he wouldn't.

'Yes, you call me "sir",' Jack said, his tone dangerously controlled. 'And you show some respect.'

Sergeyev smiled. He glanced round – checking Levin was nowhere to be seen, Rose guessed. 'Oh, I'm scared, *sir*.'

Jack smiled back. But the smile didn't reach his eyes. 'Know what scares me?'

'Everything, *sir*?'

Jack ignored him. 'I used to think I was scared by death. Or by facing death – by combat and action and the uncertainty of the battlefield. Not any more. No, now what scares me is the possibility I might live to grow old. I might wake up one day tired and wasted and unable even to open a beer. I might need crutches and a hearing aid and help getting dressed. When and if I get to that point, it'll be my memories that'll keep me going. The fact that I've lived through so much, survived so much, to get there. Do you want to get old?' he asked, prodding Sergeyev in the chest. 'Do you want to end up with only your memories to make up for the loss of your faculties?' He pointed across the room. 'Look at her. Look! She's there already. Nineteen, and she can barely walk on her own. She should be looking forward to her whole life, not staring at the end of it and wondering what happened. If she can wonder at all.'

Sergeyev didn't reply.

Jack held his gaze for a moment more, then turned away. 'Get out,' he said. 'Go and do something useful, while you still can.'

There was an embarrassed silence as the others slowly followed Sergeyev from the room. Klebanov paused to clap his hand on Jack's shoulder, as if to say he understood.

'Help yourselves to whatever you need,' he told the Doctor. 'If you want anything else, talk to Alex and he'll do what he can.'

Soon only the Doctor, Rose and Jack were left. And Valeria.

The base had been built to house fifty scientists and their equipment. With just four, it was virtually empty. Levin found several large storerooms packed with filing cabinets, which, Alex Minin explained, contained all the records from when the base was fully operational – and fully funded. Everything from payroll details to equipment requisitions and original schematics for building the place.

Minin had suggested the soldiers use the lecture hall

as their base since it was the largest room. Levin took an office on the same corridor as his headquarters. Not that he'd got anything to put there apart from his pack. But he had Minin bring him pads of paper and pencils and a large-scale map of the area.

The Doctor found him half an hour later.

'You're finished?' Levin said, waving for the Doctor to sit down opposite the desk. 'That was quick.'

'I'm not a medical man. Just a quick examination.'

'So you can tell me nothing.'

'I can tell you why there are no biros,' the Doctor said, nodding at the pencil that Levin was tapping on his fingers. 'The ink freezes in winter.'

'Then I'm glad it's only autumn. I intend to be long gone by the time winter arrives.'

'Think you'll have finished?'

'I'm only here to investigate the energy spike. We find something, we're gone. We find nothing, we're gone. This death, that poor girl – a separate matter.'

'You sure?'

'Aren't you?'

The Doctor leaned back and crossed his legs. He was an odd one, Levin thought, not for the first time. If the phones worked he'd call Moscow and get some background on him. But his paperwork seemed in excellent order. Someone must think highly of him. So Levin said, 'Tell me.'

'The dead kid – jellified. As we thought.'

'That's hardly a medical term.'

'But it's accurate. All the energy drained from the

body and the bones dissolved. The calcium seems to have been sucked out or something. Same with the girl, only to a lesser extent. I'd guess her bones are weakened and brittle. But the process is less far gone. Something interrupted it.'

'But what caused it?'

'Thought you weren't interested.'

'Not professionally.'

'Then you should be.'

'Oh, yes?'

'Oh, yes. Think about it. The energy was sucked out of those kids.'

Levin was getting bored with this. 'So?'

'So…' The Doctor uncrossed his legs and leaned forwards. 'Ask yourself. Where did it go?'

And now Levin did see. 'That energy spike? But surely there's not enough energy in two human bodies – one and a half, actually – to show up like that?'

'No, there isn't.'

'So that wasn't the source.'

'Not all of it, no. There must be something else.'

'As I said, another unrelated source.' Levin leaned back, to show the matter was closed.

'Possibly. But it might not be instead, it might be as well. Something we haven't found yet.'

Levin felt cold – even colder than he did already. 'Like…'

The Doctor was nodding encouragingly.

'Like more bodies,' Levin said.

* * *

There were two Jeeps, or the rather clunky Russian equivalents, at the base. Jack demanded a driver to take him and Valeria to her home in the village. He specifically asked for Sergeyev, though he wasn't sure why he'd done that.

He was sorry to admit to himself that if he was honest he'd be glad to get rid of the girl. OK, he felt sorry for her – no one should have to go through whatever she'd been through. But it wasn't as if she knew anything about it. Her hurting was done and there was nothing that Jack could do now. Best get her home and let her parents worry about it and sort her out.

Maybe he wanted Sergeyev to see him dust his hands of her, to see he was one of lads really. Then Levin had agreed that Jack would help organise the group taking readings with their Geiger counters and stuff. Intelligence officer was an easy role, he decided, as he sat in the back of the Jeep with the motionless girl.

Sofia Barinska agreed to drop the Doctor off at the stone circle.

'I just want to have a look,' he said. 'And Rose wants to see the village, don't you, Rose?'

'Do I?'

'Course you do.'

So they sat in the back of the large car as Sofia drove the short, bumpy way back to the stones on the cliff top.

'Why do I want to see the village?' Rose asked.

'Have a look round, ask a few questions. I dunno, see what you can find out?'

'What about?'

'You need to find that out too.'

'Dead people?'

'I don't think this is the first time it's happened. I don't think it's a coincidence it's happened now, all right?'

'All right.' She wasn't convinced.

'Anyway, it'll be fun.'

'Oh yeah?

'Yeah. Rose Tyler – Special Investigator.'

'What sort of title is that?' she said with a laugh. Then another thought occurred to her. 'Hey, why don't they think I've got a strange name? I mean, it's not very Russian, is it?'

'It's like you hearing what they say but not how they say it. What the TARDIS does for you,' the Doctor explained, keeping his voice low. They were almost at the stones now and Barinska was swinging the car in a wide arc, slowing down. 'You hear English from them, they hear Russian from you, including your name. It just sort of fits.'

'You mean, I'm like Rosetska Tylerov or something?'

'Don't look at me. I'm probably Doctorsky.'

She thought about this and laughed again.

But the Doctor was already climbing out of the car. 'See you, then.'

'Where?'

He shrugged. 'Around.' He closed the door.

'Hey, wait.' She was talking to Sofia. 'I'll join you.' Rose climbed through into the front of the car and sat down in the passenger seat. 'Thanks for the ride.'

Sofia barely glanced at her. But for the first time there was the trace of a friendly smile on her face.

He was right, it was good to be rid of the poor girl. Jack was glad it was over. He tried to joke with Sergeyev, but the Russian soldier refused to be drawn.

'Hey, look, sorry I bawled you out. I've had a bad day. I know you have too. But it's all sorted now, right?'

Sergeyev nodded without looking at him.

'Good man.' Jack grinned. 'Let's get this show on the road, then, eh?'

But as they drove off to join the rest of the squad, Jack couldn't help but remember the face of the man who'd opened the door to them. The man who had led the silent, expressionless, aged girl inside. The man who was himself aged long past his real years, but by the climate and the life he was scratching out for them both. The face of a man whose whole purpose in life had just been taken from him and replaced by a very different commitment.

A man with no hope left. And no daughter.

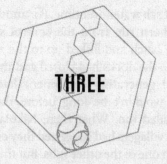

THREE

The whole submarine smelled of rust and oil and salt and diesel fuel. Nikolai Stresnev adjusted the regulator and listened to the tone of the old generator change slightly. None of the gauges worked any more, so he had to do it all from the sound the thing made.

Long ago, he used to play the violin. But the last of his strings had broken many years before and there was no chance of getting replacements. Sitting on the cold, wet metal floor beside the generator, he often thought he could hear the music echoing through the damp corridors of the old sub. But not today. Today all he could hear was the faint cry of the wind from outside. When it was from the east, it caught the conning tower, funnelled down through the open hatchway and into the structure. When there was a fierce storm, the whole sub shook and rolled, and Nikolai could feel the wind in his hair even in the generator room.

But he couldn't close the hatch behind him. For one thing, it was rusted open – the hinges welded solid by the action of salt water over time. For another, the main cables had been run from the control systems back through the hatch and linked up to the village power supply. Since the docks had closed and the troops left, the original generating equipment had failed and decayed. It wouldn't be long before this last diesel generator failed too. What then, Nikolai wondered? Some of the villagers had suggested they could fire up a generator on one of the other subs. But this was the last diesel boat – the others were all nuclear. It might work, it might even work safely. But Nikolai had made it very clear that they could find someone else to do it.

There were only two places in the village that were truly warm. This was one of them – snuggled down next to the running generator. The other was the inn on the quayside. It used to be the harbourmaster's office back in the old days. Now it was inn, community centre and town hall all rolled into one.

So when he picked up his flask and found that the last scalding drops of vodka were gone, it wasn't much of a decision where to go for the rest of the afternoon. He scratched at his ear – a rapid, jerky movement like a dog angered by fleas. The generator was running smoothly; it had a full tank and wouldn't need attention until the evening. He pulled himself to his feet and made his way along the narrow corridor, careful to duck under the exposed pipework. Rust was flaking from the walls and water dripped constantly from the ceiling. It was touch and go which gave out first – the generator or the whole infrastructure of the submarine.

The breeze bit at Nikolai's face as he reached the top of the ladder and emerged from the hatch. There were flakes of snow in the air, twisting and turning lazily on their way to the ground. He could hear the faint whistle of the breeze round the other submarines. Like mermaids singing, he used to think. Now he barely noticed it.

Except now it was different. There was something else. He paused, listening, trying to make out what the difference was – a slithering, scraping sound. Like something heavy but wet being dragged across the ice on the other side of the sub. But when he crossed the tower and leaned out to take a look, there was nothing. Just the thin, broken ice and the near-frozen water lapping gently at the rusty hulk of dark metal. Large chunks of broken ice clunked against the sides of the sub, as if the inlet was a huge glass of iced vodka.

With that thought in the front of his mind, Nikolai climbed down to the deck, jumped across to the quay and made his way past the abandoned submarines and forgotten derricks and cranes towards the inn.

It was a pleasant walk back from the stone circle to the scientific base. The institute was squat and ugly and concrete – just the sort of place you'd expect people in starched white coats to be cultivating extremely nasty biological weapons or irradiating poor guinea pigs in the name of science, the Doctor thought.

The two soldiers at the gates into the compound snapped to attention as the Doctor sauntered past. He resisted the temptation to salute and grinned happily at them instead.

Same story with the two guards at the door. It was an impressive door, riveted metal. 'That'd keep a nuclear blast out, that would,' the Doctor lied jovially. But it occurred to him that its purpose might be not to keep unpleasant things out but rather to keep them inside.

Klebanov was in what seemed to be the main laboratory. He was working alone and made a point of standing in front of the array of test tubes and flasks organised across the workbench when the Doctor came in.

'Thought you were a physicist,' the Doctor said. 'And shouldn't you have a white coat?'

'We are informal here,' Klebanov told him warily. He obviously thought the Doctor was a threat. Probably a political one.

'I'm not here to close you down, you know. You've nothing to worry about. And I'm not going to steal your research either, whatever it is.'

'I am multi-disciplinary,' Klebanov replied.

'Typical scientist,' the Doctor joked. 'Always ready with his retort.'

Klebanov didn't laugh. Maybe it lost something in translation.

The Doctor went on, 'I'm after a microscope. Ideally scanning electron. Possibly pseudo-quantum-enabled.' No response. 'With flashing lights and stuff.'

'Talk to Minin,' Klebanov told him. 'He handles the supplies.'

'And the admin,' the Doctor remarked.

'And the monkeys.'

'What?' The Doctor turned to see who had spoken.

It was Boris Brodsky, standing in the doorway behind them. He gave a short laugh. 'Just joking. He'll be in his office.'

'Ta.'

Brodsky gave the Doctor directions, while Klebanov went back to his flasks and test tubes.

The Doctor had his own test tube. Inside was lodged a tiny sliver of material he'd managed, after considerable effort, to dislodge from one of the standing stones. It looked just like rock with veins of quartz through it. Maybe that's all it was, but a microscope would tell him. He rattled the test tube to announce his presence to Minin as he walked into his office.

Alex Minin was standing at his desk, looking intently at an open folder of papers. He turned a page, looked up and, after a moment's hesitation, closed the folder. 'Can I help you, Doctor?'

'You ever heard of a pseudo-quantum microscope?'

Minin shook his head. 'I'm not a scientist. But, no, I haven't.'

'Neither have I,' the Doctor confessed. 'And I am a scientist. So if someone asked me for one I'd tell them they were talking rubbish, not send them to the stores.'

After a pause, Minin said, 'I'm sorry, was that it? Only I'm a bit…'

'Busy?' the Doctor nodded. He stepped up to the desk

and examined some of the papers beside the closed folder – requisitions and purchase orders. 'Must take a lot of time running a place like this. Three staff and you, no urgency for supplies, no one interested in sending any anyway. It's the cleaning roster that takes the time, is it?'

Minin's eyes narrowed. 'It's because no one cares that it takes the time. We have to eat, we need clothes and fuel and, yes, even brushes and mops. You'd be surprised how much we need to keep us going.'

'Yeah. I guess the difficult thing is getting the balance. Ordering enough to help the villagers while not drawing attention. Does Klebanov know?'

Minin's surprise turned into a snort of derision. 'He knows nothing.'

'You could be right about that. But tell me – why are you so unpopular?'

Minin slipped off his jacket and hung it over the back of his chair before sitting down behind the desk. The Doctor cleared a pile of books off the only other chair and sat down too. The books seemed to be logbooks and they were quite old, which was interesting.

'I was the political officer here, in the old days. It was my job to make sure everyone toed the party line. It was my job to report anyone who spoke carelessly about their work, or was seen with someone they had no business to be with, or who sneezed during the national anthem. They all quietly resented it, of course. But they couldn't complain because I reported them for that too.'

'And now they openly resent it.'

'Wouldn't you?'

He opened a drawer and took out two small glasses and a half-empty bottle of vodka. As he reached in, his sleeve pulled back and the Doctor could see a dark mark on his arm – the edge of a tattoo.

'So why stay here?'

'No one wanted me back in Moscow. Easier to leave me here and forget about me. I have no skills apart from betraying the trust of my fellows.'

'Oh, don't belittle yourself.' The Doctor accepted the glass of clear liquid and examined it. 'What about despondency, regret, depression?'

'I can do those too,' Minin admitted. He knocked back his vodka and grimaced at the taste and the burn in his throat. 'I wanted to be a teacher,' he said quietly.

'We're all teachers,' the Doctor told him. 'I'd like to learn about this.' He held up the test tube. 'So I need a microscope. The bigger and flashier the better.'

'Shouldn't be a problem.' Minin picked up the bottle. He hesitated a moment, then shoved it back into the drawer. 'Why are you here, Doctor?'

'Microscope.'

'That's not what I meant.'

'I know.'

'And?'

The Doctor shrugged. 'I dunno. Like you, I'm interested in history. I want to help.'

'History? How did you…' Minin's face cleared. 'Ah – the logbooks.'

'And the maps and the notebooks and the file you don't want me to see.'

'It's what I do to pass the time,' Minin admitted. 'I've researched the history of Novrosk ever since I came here. Needed something to hide in, an escape.'

'Interesting?'

'Yes, actually.' Minin's face seemed to come to life with enthusiasm as he leaned across the desk. 'Before the navy came, this was an old whaling station, you know. Some of the villagers still here can trace their ancestry back to those original whalers. Or rather, they could if they bothered.'

'Lots of colour, lots of local background,' the Doctor suggested.

Minin was nodding in agreement.

'Lots of local legends?'

Minin froze. 'Ah. You know.'

'I do now. Lucky guess. Something Barinska said. Tell me about the Vourdulak.'

Minin stood up, his hand at his mouth as if ready to catch any unconsidered words. 'It's just a story,' he said at last. 'The sort of legend that springs up in any community like this – isolated and old. Probably there's some truth, some event, at the root of it. An unfortunate accident, an unexplained death that they tried to rationalise.'

'Go on.'

'The locals believe that somewhere on the peninsula is a Vourdulak, a sort of vampire. Actually more like a siren – a seemingly beautiful young girl who entraps the unwary and then drains their energy to keep herself young and beautiful, whereas in fact she is old and ugly…'

'So what happened to Valeria is a bit of a shock. The legend comes home to roost.'

'They know it's just a story,' Minin countered. 'They've serviced and repaired the most advanced and dangerous weapons in the world down here. They're living with the remains of them rotting away within sight. They don't really believe in this thing, this monster. They know there's a proper explanation for what's happened. It's just that no one has found it yet.'

The Doctor waited, but Minin seemed to have said his piece and sat down again.

'Is that what they think? Or what you think?' the Doctor wondered. 'And if it's just a story and this is unexpected and unconnected, what's in that file?'

Minin did not reply. Instead he picked up the file, weighed it in his hand and then passed it across the desk to the Doctor.

'It's the post-mortem and military police report from when it happened while the base was fully open. A corpse drained of all binding energy and with the bones turned to slush.'

The Doctor opened the file and leafed through the pages gathered inside.

'And also copies of local police records for the twenty years before that,' Minin said.

There were photocopies of handwritten reports and

pages from ledgers. A telegram, yellowed and brittle with age.

'Accounts of the original legends. A letter from one of the whalers to his sister in St Petersburg describing a death in 1827. All manner of other reports and descriptions from local records, journals. Even a page of a log from one of the submarines, together with the order of transfer for the captain who was foolish enough to write it.'

The Doctor held up a single page printed out from a computer file. The printer had been almost out of ink by the look of it. 'And this.' It wasn't a question.

'And that, yes. It was ignored, of course. Like the rest. Sofia Barinska's report from two years ago. From last time it happened.'

Rose's attempts to engage Sofia Barinska in conversation met with little response. The woman's mind was obviously on other things, though whether it was the unexpected arrival of three dozen soldiers together with the Doctor, Jack and Rose or the unexplained attacks on two young people was not clear. Probably a bit of both, Rose decided.

'So, you grew up here?' she tried.

'Here, you are born grown-up,' Sofia replied.

Well, it was a start.

'I guess it's tough.'

This earned a sideways look as the car bumped over the join between two enormous slabs of concrete. The road seemed to have been dumped and left to fend for itself. Grass was poking through the crumbling surface. There were no visible lines or markings at all.

'You could just leave,' Rose said quietly. She could hear the frustration in her own voice and she didn't even live here.

'I'll catch the next train,' Sofia said, her voice devoid of emotion.

'There's a station?'

'Not any more. The last train left over twenty years ago.'

'Oh. Right… Where are we going?'

Sofia did look at her now, and for longer than Rose thought was probably safe as they bumped across the decaying road surface. 'First to the police station, which is also my house, to check for messages. Then I have to tell Pavel's parents what has happened,' she said. 'After that, even if you don't, I'll need a drink.'

The Doctor read through the autopsy report at a glance. He flicked through the other papers and then handed the file back to Minin.

'Aren't you going to read it all?'

'I have read it all.'

'And?'

'And I think you'd need to exhume one of the bodies and examine it to be sure the cause of death is the same.'

'It sounds the same. Anyway,' Minin went on, putting the file away in a drawer of his desk, 'you can't go digging up old bodies, not without a permit. You'd need permission from Barinska and the next of kin at least. Otherwise it's illegal.'

'And sucking out people's bones and life essence isn't?'

Minin sighed. 'You know what I mean.'

'I know what you mean. Now, where's that microscope?'

Minin sent the Doctor to find Catherine Kornilova. She had her own lab on the other side of the building, with equipment including a powerful electron microscope, Minin assured him. To get there the Doctor had to take the corridor that ran just inside the outer wall of the large building. Strangely there didn't seem to be any way to cut through the middle.

She was sitting at a workbench tapping away at the keyboard of a laptop computer when the Doctor arrived. He watched her for a moment from the door before stepping into the room. Mid-twenties, dark hair tied back, white lab coat. She was wearing glasses that had a string attached so they would hang round her neck when she didn't need them. A sensible, practical woman.

'All mod cons,' he observed.

She didn't look up. 'Hardly the latest model, but it serves.' She finished the sentence she was typing, then looked up and smiled. 'What can I do for you, Doctor?'

'Come to beg the use of a microscope.'

'Help yourself.' She nodded across at the equipment set up on a table at the side of the room. 'Again, it's hardly the latest model, but it should do. What do you want it for?'

'Want to look at this.' The Doctor held up the sliver of rock in its glass tube. 'From one of the standing stones.'

'Granite, with quartz embedded in it.'

'You know that for a fact?'

'Seems likely.' She closed the lid of the laptop and came over to join him at the microscope. 'You need a hand?'

'Thanks.'

'Mind you, I'm a biologist not a geologist.'

'Really?' The Doctor put down his rock sample. 'So, tell me about the monkeys.'

She hesitated only a second, but it was a hesitation nonetheless. 'There are no monkeys.'

'Oh?'

'Never have been.'

'Really? Then why do Boris and the others keep mentioning them?'

'They're teasing Alex. I wish they'd leave him alone. Here, let me do that.'

She took the rock sample and started to prepare a slide, reaching for a scalpel to scrape away a surface layer for examination.

'So what's the big joke?'

'They're just getting at Alex for his pedantry. He's always after them for filling in forms and getting reports submitted on time and in the right format. Well, that's fine by me – he's right. If we give those clowns in Moscow any excuse they'll ignore us. But Klebanov and Boris and the villagers who remember how things used to be, they resent Alex even being here. There was even a death apparently. A suicide. So they take the mickey whenever they can, right?'

'Right.' The Doctor watched as she adjusted the controls and an image spluttered into view on a monitor screen – a picture of the fragment of rock sample. It looked pitted and cratered like a lunar landscape. 'And the monkeys?'

'Before my time. And Boris's. Apparently Alex found some paperwork for a few live specimens. He went ape, if you'll forgive the expression.' She smiled at her own choice of words.

'An ethical man.'

'Oh, I don't think he cared what happened to the monkeys. He was just annoyed because the paperwork was all done and the money was taken out of the budget, but there were never any monkeys. No delivery. No one even seemed to know who'd sent the order in the first place or why.'

'Biological weapons research,' the Doctor said. 'You're a biologist, you can guess why they wanted them.'

'I'm not that sort of biologist,' she snapped. 'I'm researching vaccines and counter-biological agents.'

'Course you are. That's why it's all so secret.'

'That's why it's all so makeshift and amateur,' she replied. 'Anyway, Alex kicked up a fuss about nonexistent monkeys and they've never let him forget it. I think it was the same week that Chedakin died. Maybe that's why.'

The Doctor had turned his attention to the screen

and was magnifying the image. 'Yeah, maybe.' There was something odd here, he thought. The impurities in the stone that everyone assumed were quartz... They didn't look like random strata, more as if they had been deliberately laid into the base stone. 'That remind you of anything?'

Catherine shrugged. 'Not really. I suppose it looks a bit like a printed circuit.'

'That's what I thought. Standing stones that are really silicon chips?' He clicked his tongue and changed the magnification again. 'So, who was Chedakin?'

Rose stayed in the car, cold despite being out of the wind. Sofia had the heater on full, but it didn't seem to take the chill out of the air. They had parked behind a digger – a big JCB-type job. It was the first vehicle apart from Sofia's that Rose had seen and, like everything else, it was rusty and old.

She watched the policewoman at the door of the little square house, talking to the man and woman – Pavel's parents. It was difficult to watch, but even more difficult to look away. The woman was crying, the man with his arm round her and his own face ashen-grey.

Then Sofia returned, and she drove in silence for a while. 'I'm going to the inn,' she said at last.

'You're right, we need a drink. You need a drink.' Rose struggled for something to say. 'What's the inn called?'

'Doesn't have a name. It's just the inn.'

'Right. It can't be easy, your line of work.'

'Easy? Usually it's boringly easy. But some days...'

'How did they take it?'

'Badly. But we're used to death and hardship out here.' Sofia's eyes were focused on the cracked road stretching ahead. The derelict cranes and gantries at the docks were looming closer, dark against the steel-grey of the sky. 'Vahlen – Pavel's father – his best friend was Chedakin. So for him it's another loss.'

'What happened to Chedakin?'

'He died,' she said.

The inn was just ahead of them now as they drove along the old quay. It was a square, concrete building distinguished from its neighbours only by the fact that there was light rather than wooden boards in the windows.

Sofia stopped in the middle of the roadway outside the door. Since hers was the only car, she could presumably park wherever she liked. In this case, next to a rusting submarine, its conning tower thrust up from the icy waters beside the quay.

'He shot himself.' The evening was drawing in now. 'He used to say what he really thought, not what he was *supposed* to think. We found it refreshing. But we kept warning him, everyone did.'

The sudden sound of laughter from the inn as they approached seemed out of place in the dreary, grey desolation.

'What happened?'

Sofia was ahead of Rose and didn't look back. 'He was ordered to Moscow, due to leave the next day. They were sending a helicopter for him. He killed himself rather than face that.'

'But how did they know?' It seemed such a different world – where you could be taken away and locked up, or worse, simply for speaking your mind. Rose couldn't imagine herself or the Doctor surviving long in such an environment. And God help her mum.

'Same way they always knew.' The bitterness and anger were palpable in her voice. 'Alex Minin told them.'

On the other side of the docks, away from the noise of the inn, the water lapped gently and icily against the crumbling quay. The dry dock where the submarines were refitted and their hulls examined for weak spots and corrosion was flooded and useless. One of the subs was lying on its side in the water, having rusted through and toppled over several years before. It was held up only by the dark hulk of the next submarine.

Beyond this, there was a narrow beach of shingle, then the jutting cliff at the edge of the bay. The sea pounded against the base of the cliff, gradually wearing it away. Eventually it would carve out so much rock that the land would crash down into the sea, pushing the cliff back towards the stone circle.

Sergeyev had taken Jack to where the rest of his squad were waiting, at the edge of the docks. They were split into teams of three men, each team having a Geiger counter.

'The colonel and the Doctor don't think that it's a radiation leak, so there should be no danger,' Jack said before Sergeyev could speak. Time to assert his authority. 'But we have to check to eliminate the possibility.'

'There's a lot of background radiation, sir,' one of the soldiers said. He turned on the Geiger counter and it immediately started clicking. 'Not enough to worry about at the moment, but if it gets any higher…'

'How far have you got?' Sergeyev asked him, while glaring at Jack.

'We checked the warehouses on this side of the quay. Also the dry dock, though it is not dry any more.'

'Inside the subs?' Jack asked.

The soldiers shook their heads. There was little enthusiasm at the thought.

'We probably don't need to go inside,' Sergeyev pointed out. 'We can take readings from outside the hull.'

Jack thought about this. 'OK. But anything above the expected background, we check. Right?'

Grudging nods. So Jack repeated, 'Right?'

'Sir.'

'It'll be dark soon, so let's get started.'

The evening was drawing in fast. So if anyone had seen the dark shape that dragged itself out of the water and across the shingle they might have dismissed it as creeping shadow. If anyone had heard the sound of the creature hauling itself up onto the crumbling quayside, they might have dismissed that as the waves breaking on the rocks below the cliff.

But the soldiers had moved away. So there was no one there to make such a mistake. No one to see the tentacles probing and stretching and exploring. No one to hear the creature's hiss of satisfaction as it slithered along the quay.

FOUR

The room was noisy and filled with smoke, like the local pub on football nights. The sound dipped a little as Rose and Sofia entered, but news of the arrivals had already travelled round the community so it was only a pause, not a full-blown silence of surprise. Rose had half expected to be told, 'We don't want strangers here,' so she was relieved that everyone settled back to their drinks and conversations.

Sofia led Rose through to an empty table near the back of the room. She waved at the burly man behind the bar as she went, and moments later two glasses and a bottle were slammed down on the table.

'Is it true?' the barman demanded. His voice was gruff and hoarse.

'I can't say,' Sofia told him, pouring the drinks.

'Thought so.'

The man heaved a sigh and made his way back to the bar, collecting empty glasses and bottles as he went.

'News travels fast,' Rose said.

'There's nothing much to do apart from gossip. Not once the boats are back in for the evening.'

'Boats?'

'Fishing boats. We can get to the open sea from the far end of the harbour, even when it's iced up.'

That explained the smell, then. Rose looked round. Not surprisingly, she found that a lot of people were looking back at her. Most of them were men, but there were a few women too. Everyone looked tired and worn. What a life, she thought – get up, go out on a fishing boat or dig in the fields, then get hammered and flop into bed.

'Doesn't it ever get warm here?' she asked.

Sofia pointed to the drink – a small glass of pale liquid. 'Drink that, it'll make you warm. Or as close as you can get.'

Rose drank it. The sound of her rasping, breathless cough made Sofia laugh. Pretty soon the people at the closest tables were laughing too, and then the next ones, and everyone. Finally, when she could, Rose laughed. Her eyes were brimming over with the tears the burning liquid had brought out.

'Next time I'll have a coffee,' she gasped.

The Doctor had been staring at the screen for what seemed like hours. Catherine went back to her laptop and finished her report. He was still staring at the screen, though he had changed the magnification again.

'Fascinating, this,' he announced.

'Still at it, then?' She shut down the computer and wandered back over to the microscope.

'Can I see a different sample, make sure they're the same?' he asked.

'Sure.'

Catherine removed the glass specimen case from the microscope. She opened it up and carefully took out the thin sliver of stone with a pair of tweezers. But the stone slipped from between the prongs and fell onto the workbench. She picked it up with her fingers.

And the world swam.

For a moment she was giddy, vision blurred, swaying on her feet. Then she dropped the tiny piece of stone. She felt the Doctor taking her arm, sitting her on a lab stool.

'You all right?'

'I think so.' Her vision was clearing now. 'Just... tired, I suppose.' Her thumb and fingers felt numb, where she had held the stone. She stared down at them, rubbing them together, trying to focus. 'Oh, my God – my fingers!'

'Let's have a look.' The Doctor took her hand in his and examined it. 'I see what you mean.'

The tips of her fingers and her thumb were wrinkled, the skin creased as if she'd been in the bath too long. The fingers of an old woman.

The Doctor was reaching for the tiny fragment of stone. Instinctively she knew that it was the fragment that had somehow done this to her.

'Don't!'

But he already had it. He turned it over in his palm, flipped it in the air and caught it in his other hand before replacing it in the test tube with the larger piece. Then he showed her his hand. The palm was withered, the skin on the fingers slack and dry and ancient.

'What's going on here?' Klebanov had come in without them noticing and was looking accusingly at the Doctor. 'I hope you're not wasting my staff's time.'

'Don't think so. We're fine, ta. Thanks for asking. Answering questions, and asking lots more.'

'I wish you would take things seriously and speak with due respect,' Klebanov huffed.

Catherine was surprised he was so annoyed – it wasn't as if there was any urgency to their work, or the Doctor was stopping her getting on. And now…

The Doctor was still holding up his hand. It seemed to be healing, the skin tightening again. But Catherine's own fingers remained wrinkled and parched. She held out her hand to show him, wondering what had happened, surprised at her dispassionate scientific curiosity about the change to her own body.

Klebanov came over to the workbench. He leaned forwards, his weight on his hands on the bench, eyes closed.

The Doctor took hold of Catherine's hand and examined it. 'You feel all right?' he asked.

Before Catherine could answer, Klebanov opened his eyes and straightened up. 'Yep,' he said. 'Ta. Thanks for asking.'

* * *

There was quite a crowd round the table now. Rose had managed to fend off questions about life in the rest of Russia and the political situation in Moscow. The villagers were more than happy to unburden themselves and tell her how awful their own lives were.

Actually, though, she sensed that most of the problem was resentment at having been abandoned when the docks were decommissioned. They were surviving, they got essential supplies from the research institute and the fishermen and farmers provided enough food.

Except for the recent death, and what had happened to Valeria. No one said so specifically, but Rose had the clear impression that this wasn't the first time unexpected and unexplained death had come to Novrosk. If she'd to make a bet she would guess that having more than a dozen rotting nuclear submarines in the middle of the community didn't do a whole lot for health and safety, but then again it seemed that the subs were also the saviour of the community.

The only way they got any power, Sofia told Rose, was by keeping the generator on one of the submarines going. 'Don't worry, it's diesel not nuclear,' she added, seeing Rose's look of horror. She then introduced Rose to Nikolai Stresnev, who proudly told her he serviced and worked the generator and kept it going.

Stresnev was typical of so many of the men in the community – prematurely aged, tired, borderline drunk. He lived for the moment and had a habit of scratching furiously at his ear like an irritated dog. Rose tried not to think about why he might do that and what sort of provision he made for personal hygiene. So far as she could tell, he practically lived on the submarine. Except when he was at the inn.

She tried to steer the conversation back to the deaths, hoping to find out if there really had been other similar events and if so how recently. 'Doesn't it scare you?' she asked when no one seemed especially bothered.

'People die,' Sofia explained. 'It's a hard life. We lose a few fishermen every year. Flu takes others – we've no medical facilities… And we live with the subs and what might happen to them.'

'But that's frightening.'

'Only if you stop to think about it. We live with it all the time. You get used to it. Like anything.'

'If you want to be really frightened,' Nikolai said, pointing vaguely in Rose's direction, 'you should go and visit old Georgi. He's seen some things.'

'Really? What's he seen, then?'

'Ignore him,' Sofia said. 'Georgi's old and blind. Lost his sight way back. An accident servicing one of the boats back in the navy days.'

'He still sees things,' Nikolai insisted. 'Things that haven't happened yet, and all.' He drained his glass and slammed it back down on the table. 'That's why they call it *second* sight.'

'He's a poor, blind old man,' Sofia insisted.

Rose nodded. 'So, where's he live?' she asked.

When the Doctor refused to be intimidated by

Klebanov and countered his criticisms with the vague suggestion that he'd talk to his mates in Moscow and see what they reckoned, Klebanov left them to it.

'He's not usually so huffy,' Catherine assured the Doctor.

'He's usually in charge,' the Doctor told her. 'Look at that.' He showed her his hand. It seemed to be back to normal. Catherine's was still wrinkled and aged. 'You'll have to moisturise,' the Doctor said sympathetically. 'But the tissue round it is in good shape. I think it'll recover in a few days. Your body'll sort it out.'

'But what happened? And why, when it affected you, did your skin recover straight away?'

The Doctor shook his head. 'Makes no sense,' he muttered. 'I mean, energy absorption – OK, lots of reasons you'd want to do that. But you'd never be daft enough to tune it just to one strain of DNA and life force. Why just humans, eh? I mean, I'm close, so if it won't take me it won't take anything else. Accept no substitutes – what's that about?'

Catherine laughed nervously, staring at her wrinkled fingers. 'I have no idea what you're talking about.'

He laughed with her. 'Nor me. But think about it. You need energy, so you absorb it – through these stones. And the quartz-like substance also resonates like quartz. That's what sends the signal. But they don't do it all the time. You don't, like, lean on a stone and – *pow* – you're 107 years old and spineless. So they must be activated somehow. Radiation from the microscope might have set it off.'

'We're not short of radiation round here,' Catherine replied slowly. 'It's a worry, but you get used to living with it. Despite what the surveys and the official reports say. Some of those subs are leaking like… like…' She struggled to think of a simile.

'Like rusty old submarines?' the Doctor suggested. 'But you wouldn't just want energy from humans, would you? You'd take whatever you can get.'

'Depends what you need it for, maybe.'

He frowned as if she'd just told him two plus two made five. 'I know what they need it for,' he said.

Georgi Zinoviev was sitting alone in the dark when Sofia Barinska brought the English girl to see him. No one else knew she was English and her accent was perfect. It wasn't from the way she spoke that Georgi knew. He just did. And he knew that she didn't want anyone else to know, so he sent Sofia away, back to the inn while they spoke.

'I never put the lights on,' he confessed. 'Why would I bother? So you'll have to find the switch. If there is one.'

'Don't you get visitors?' she asked.

'Not many. A few. One day the man with the wolf on his arm will come.'

'A wolf?' Rose felt suddenly cold – even colder than she had already been. 'Why?'

She meant why would he have a wolf on his arm, but that wasn't the question the old man answered. 'To kill me,' he said. 'Please sit down.'

'That's weird. How did you know I haven't?'

'I may be blind, but I still see pictures in my head. And when you speak, I can sense where the sound is coming from. So I know you are not sitting.'

'They say you can see… things.'

He laughed. 'I know what they say. Maybe they are right. Even I have stopped listening to my stories now. The rest of them gave up listening to my stories, to what I saw happening, long ago.'

'Because you got it wrong?' she asked.

He laughed again, but there was no humour in it. 'No. Because I got it right.'

'You can see the future?'

'Oh, no. I can only see the present, just like you. Except that, unlike you, I don't need my eyes to see it. I don't even need to be there.'

'So what do you see now?'

'It's not something I choose to do, you know.'

'Sorry.'

'That's all right. But…' He hesitated. There was something, something stirring at the edge of his mind. 'I see ripples in the water. Broken ice and tracks in the snow. The soldiers are there – on the quay.'

They were working their way steadily along the quay. Jack had kept Sergeyev in the same team with him – along with another soldier called Razul. It was Razul who had the Geiger counter, swinging it in an arc in front of him as they walked. They could all hear its insistent clicking.

* * *

'And Nikolai is leaving the inn. He's drunk, of course, but the generator will need more diesel soon. And he's tired and cold, so he's looking forward to sleeping.'

The officer who was with the soldiers but wore no uniform watched the man swaying along the quay, heard him grunt a few words to the soldiers before he set off towards one of the subs. The man was walking as if he was on a ship that was pitching on a stormy sea.

'And there is someone else. Something else. Waiting in the dark.'

Nikolai had almost reached the sub when he heard it – a faint crackling like electricity, combined with a wet, slithering sound. Like something heavy being dragged across the concrete behind him. But when he looked, there was nothing there. Just shadows.

'Hunting. Waiting for the right moment.'

There were a few lights still working along the quay. They only bothered to replace the bulbs in the lamps as far as the inn, and a few between the inn and the sub for Nikolai's benefit. Between the pools of pale light they cast were islands of darkness. The lamp closest to Nikolai flickered, sputtered and died.

'Waiting for the dark.'

It unsettled him. He could feel the cold biting into his bones despite the alcohol that usually numbed his senses. He quickened his pace. And it seemed that the slithering sound was getting quicker as well. Quicker and closer.

'Waiting to strike.'

It was wet and slimy, like seaweed. Wrapping round his neck and throat. Tightening. Choking. Nikolai clawed at it, ripped at it with his nails as he fought for breath. But the strength seemed to be leaving his arms. As if he was drifting off to sleep. He could feel himself slipping away. Then more of the tentacles slapped at him, grabbing and holding and pulling.

'Waiting to kill.'

Sapping his strength and killing the scream before it left his mouth. He sank to his knees, toppled sideways. Felt himself being dragged away.

'And poor Nikolai doesn't know what's happening. He only knows one thing.'

The last thought he had was that someone needed to see to the generator. Then the darkness closed in around him and his mind was sinking into oblivion.

'That without him the generator will stop.'

Rose listened, transfixed, on the edge of her seat. The old man was staring apparently into space, except his eyes were completely white. Unseeing. Just a story, she told herself – he couldn't really know. This couldn't really be happening.

The lamp flickered, like lightning, casting shadows across Georgi's lined face, as he said, 'And the lights will go out.'

And the lights went out.

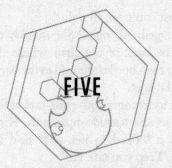

FIVE

The door to the inn crashed open. Everyone turned to stare – and saw Rose's haunted face as she looked round for Sofia Barinska. The room was lit now with flickering candles.

The policewoman was with her in a moment, the glazed look in her eyes gone. 'What's wrong? Is it old Georgi?'

Rose was gasping for breath. 'Oh, I'm so unfit it's not true. Where's Nikolai – where's the boiler bloke?'

'Gone back to the boiler. To the sub.' She nodded at the nearest candle. 'Not before time, either.'

'Probably let it run dry,' someone called out. 'Wouldn't be the first time.'

'Not that Nikolai ever runs dry,' someone else added, to general amusement.

'We have to find him.' Rose was pulling at Sofia's arm. 'Come on.'

'Why – what's wrong?'

'Georgi saw… Well, not saw exactly but…' Rose shook

her head. 'Just come on, all right?'

Sofia shrugged. 'All right.' She quickly collected her coat from the back of the chair where she had been sitting. 'Keep me a bottle,' she said to the barman. 'I think I might need it later.'

'You want us to come with you?' one of the fisherman asked Rose as she waited impatiently. His speech was slurred and it looked to her as if he'd have trouble standing up. 'Keep you safe, eh?'

'I'll be safer without your help,' she told him.

His friends laughed, and went back to their drinks.

'Tell me what happened,' Sofia said as soon as they were outside.

Snow was falling again – large, lazy flakes – as she led the way briskly towards the sub where Nikolai should be working. She was silent after hearing Rose's story.

'Look, I know it's weird, but better safe than sorry. And the lights did go out,' Rose finished, almost apologetically.

They passed between two of the huge submarines – dark shapes thrusting out of the water like beached whales in the gloom of the night. Sofia's small torch was the only light apart from the pale glow of the moon breaking through straggly clouds and shining off the snow.

'Are they just going to leave these things here?' Rose wondered, staring up at the huge, dark shapes on either side of them.

'Like us, they are left to rot. Forgotten. They grow old, waste away, die.' She stopped and reached out towards the submarine. 'Feel it.'

'What?'

'Go on.' Sofia ran the palm of her hand across the hull of the boat.

Rose copied the movement. It was rough, like sandpaper, and her hand came away dark with flakes of rust.

'That hull used to be smooth and polished and young.' Sofia was looking intently at Rose through the near-darkness. 'And now… It's like you and me, isn't it?'

'What do you mean?'

'Your skin – so smooth and perfect.'

'You should see me first thing.'

'But one day it will be like mine. Dry and ageing and wrinkled.'

'You're not doing so badly,' Rose said. 'I mean, how old are you?'

Sofia laughed. 'You wouldn't guess to look at me,' she said. Despite the laugh, there was an underlying bitterness to her tone. 'Come on, let's find Nikolai.'

It was more like a tunnel than a ship, Jack thought. The light from the three men's torches picked out ancient ironwork. A layer of rust covered everything and their feet splashed into water that dripped constantly from every pipe and seal.

The soldier with the Geiger counter walked between Sergeyev and Jack, his torch on the meter as he watched the needle judder and quiver.

'Anything?' Sergeyev asked.

'Slightly above the background level outside. Just an old reactor wanting attention.'

'Don't we all,' Jack murmured.

'This is a waste of time,' Sergeyev complained.

He was right, though Jack was loath to admit it. 'How much further to the reactor?' Jack asked.

'How should I know? I'm not a submariner.'

'I believe they are at the back of the boat,' Razul said.

'Boat?'

'Submarines are not ships, they are boats,' Razul replied. 'I know. My cousin was on the *Kursk*.'

'Poor devil,' Sergeyev said quietly.

'What happened to the *Kursk*?' Jack asked.

Razul looked up, his surprise at the question evident even in the pale light from the torches. 'It sank.'

Submarines do that, Jack thought. But he didn't say it. Instead he said, 'Oh, yes. I'm sorry. I'm surprised this thing hasn't sunk.'

'It will,' Sergeyev told him. 'And I don't want to be on it when it does. Sir,' he added, as an afterthought.

'All right. We'll head back to the quay. How are the others doing?'

They turned round in the narrow corridor. Jack was wondering how people managed to work on such a small vessel – never mind live there. The main corridor had rooms off it at intervals, but they were tiny, cramped, cluttered with pipes and cables and equipment. As if the crew had been an afterthought.

Sergeyev was talking into his lapel mike, tapping at his earpiece. 'Must be the hull of this thing, deadening the signal,' he said. 'I can't raise any of them.'

'We'll try again once we're outside,' Jack decided. 'Readings still OK?'

'I'd rather they were lower, but they're what I'd expect,' Razul reported.

Jack could feel the ladder rusting away under his feet. A constant snowfall of dust and grit and oxidised metal fell into his face from Razul above him. But Jack stayed close – he wouldn't put it past Sergeyev to slam the hatch shut as soon as Razul was out, leaving him trapped inside.

But Sergeyev was already down on the dockside, talking urgently into his mike. As Razul and Jack joined him, he shook his head. 'Still nothing, sir.' Now that there was a possible problem, he was the complete professional – all surliness gone.

'Recommendations?' Jack snapped.

'We should check on them physically.'

'You mean go and look?'

'Yes, sir. I mean go and look.'

'Except we don't know where they are,' Razul pointed out. 'One group went to the dry dock, another headed south. But where they are now…' He shrugged.

'See if they've checked in with Colonel Levin,' Jack said. 'Maybe it's us who have the communications problem, not them.'

But before Sergeyev could do that, they heard the scream. It cut through the icy air from close by – perhaps the other side of the submarine. Ear-splitting and abrupt. A shriek of surprise and fear in the night. It chilled Jack more than the cold air.

'That was Rose,' he said out loud, as he started to run.

She felt such a wimp. She felt even more of a wimp when Jack and the two soldiers came running and she ran to hug Jack. It made things slightly better that Sofia was staring horrified at the shapeless mass on the edge of the quay. But not much.

'Are you OK?'

She nodded. 'It's just the shock.' Should she tell him about old Georgi? Where should she start?

Sofia and the other soldiers were examining the body.

'Is it…' Rose couldn't go on.

Sofia nodded. 'It is Nikolai. Just as you said.'

Sergeyev shone his torch into the face. Or rather what had been the face. He quickly turned the light aside. 'Like the boy in the stone circle,' he told them. 'The body is like jelly.'

Jack took a moment to check that Rose was all right and, when she assured him she was, he joined the two soldiers. 'Did you manage to get Levin?'

Sergeyev shook his head. 'There's just static. Like interference. Or jamming.'

'Deliberate?'

'Who can say?'

'It's not the radiation,' the other soldier said. 'Not enough of it for that level of interference.'

'Then we're on our own,' Jack told them. 'We'd better try to find the others.'

'Do you know anything about generators?' Sofia asked.

'Why?'

'Because the lights have gone out,' Rose said. 'Nikolai was on his way to stoke the generator, or whatever you do with it. It provides all the power for the village.'

'Where is it?' Sergeyev asked.

'On the *Rykov*,' Sofia said. She pointed to the vast looming shadow of a submarine fifty metres down the quay. 'We ran cables from there to the old generating plant when it packed up.'

'I'm an engineer,' Razul said. 'I'll see what I can do.'

'We stick together,' Jack decided. 'There's something out here that isn't very pleasant. No one is to be alone, got that?' He looked at Rose and then Sofia. 'Are you two OK to get back to the inn and warn people?'

'Warn them?' Sofia shook her head. 'There will be panic. They will blame the Vourdulak.'

'Tell them what you have to, but tell them something.'

'We'll manage,' Rose assured him. 'Come on.'

'I'll find you at the inn,' Jack called after them. 'Then we should tell the Doctor.'

Alex Minin looked up from his paperwork to find the Doctor sitting in the chair on the other side of his desk. He gave a gasp of surprise.

'Didn't mean to startle you,' the Doctor said. Though his grin suggested he'd in fact meant to do just that.

'Can I help you?'

'Well, I've frightened Catherine and miffed Klebanov. So that leaves you and Boris.'

'And why not go to Boris?'

'He's less likely to have a spade.'

Alex put down his pen and leaned back in his chair. Somehow he got the feeling he wasn't going to like the answer to his next question. But he asked it anyway. 'And why, Doctor, do you need a spade?'

'Oh, nothing much. Just a bit of grave-robbing, you know.'

Alex swallowed. 'The previous victims?'

The Doctor was nodding excitedly. 'You can come with me if you want.'

'Doctor, it's the middle of the night. Never mind the dubious legality of the enterprise.'

'Nothing dubious about it. Completely illegal. No problem. Anyway,' he went on as he stood up, 'I need you to show me the graves. Come on, if you're coming.'

Alex stood up as well. 'Do I have a choice?'

'Nope.'

'I thought not.'

They were perhaps halfway back to the inn. With no light, it was hard to tell how far they had come and to Rose's untrained eye all the submarines looked the same.

'What will you tell them?'

Sofia seemed preoccupied, lost in her thoughts, and Rose had to ask twice before she got an answer.

'To stay indoors as much as possible and not to go out alone. Even in daylight.'

'Let's hope that's enough.'

Sofia did not reply. She stopped and raised her hand for Rose to be quiet. They were both hardly more than silhouettes against the snowy harbour road. Rose was about to ask what was wrong, but then she heard it too.

A slithering, scraping sound. Like something heavy being dragged across the road somewhere ahead of them. There was a faint mist now. The breeze had dropped and the cold night air was damp and clammy. It seemed to seep through Rose's coat and clothes and into her skin.

'What is it?' she asked in a whisper.

'I don't know.' Sofia was looking round, trying to identify exactly where the sound was coming from. 'You wait here.' She shone her torch into the misty darkness, though to little effect.

'Not likely,' Rose told her.

But then Sofia did something odd. Odd and strangely unsettling. She scratched at her ear – a rapid movement, jerky, like a dog irritated by fleas. There was no reason why she shouldn't do it, nothing strange about the gesture at all. But it made Rose feel suddenly cold and alone. She wished she'd stayed with Jack and the soldiers. And when Sofia walked cautiously into the mist, in the direction of the sound that was now fading into the night, Rose stayed exactly where she was.

Sofia Barinska's muffled footsteps faded into the mist, just as her shape had moments earlier. Rose was left alone on the quayside, hugging her arms round her body in an effort to keep warm. She stamped her feet and blew out long breaths of air that added to the thickening mist.

After what seemed like an age, Rose called out, 'Sofia? Sofia! Are you there? Stop mucking about and come back here, I can't see a thing.'

The sound was from behind her this time. The same slippery sound, like a weight of seaweed being pulled across the quay. Rose peered into the mist, but she could hardly even see the ground at her feet now that the moon was obscured. She moved slowly, cautiously, towards the sound.

Something was glowing faintly ahead of her. The light was blurred and unfocused in the mist. A torch, maybe? Jack and the soldiers returning? But if so, why hadn't the lights come back on? Or maybe they had. Rose remembered how few of the lights on the dock actually worked anyway. With the mist as well, the power might have come back on without her knowing. She continued to move cautiously forwards. The sound was still there, the light was getting brighter – blue, pulsing, eerie.

'Do I want to do this?' she asked herself quietly. The answer was probably no, but she kept going. Until her foot met something and she almost lost her balance.

Rose knelt down, partly to see what was lying at her feet and partly to stop herself from falling over it. Even so, she could barely make out the dark shape. She prodded gently with her hand. Even through her thick glove she could feel that whatever it was seemed soft and slightly springy. Like a deflating balloon.

Like jelly.

With a sharp intake of cold breath, Rose was on her feet and backing away.

In front of her the pulsing, throbbing pale-blue light moved suddenly forwards – coming straight at her.

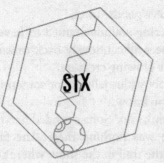

SIX

Whatever the light was, it made a slippery, slithering sound as it came. Something slapped past Rose, brushing her shoulder before flopping down on the ground at her feet. There was another sound now – something dragging. The body she had found being pulled back, towards the light that was now brighter, pulsing more rapidly. A tendril of glowing blue swept in front of Rose, making her dodge sideways and stagger backwards.

She didn't wait to see any more of the creature. She turned and ran. Straight into a dark shape that solidified out of the mist and held her tight.

'What is it?' Sofia demanded as Rose pulled away.

'There's… something. Back there.'

'What sort of something?'

Rose gave a short laugh. 'A nasty something. I didn't hang around to find out any more. And another body, I think.'

'You think?'

'Well, you've got the torch.'

The slithering sounds seemed to have stopped and Rose led the way cautiously back towards where she had seen the glowing creature.

'Like a blobby blue jellyfish or something. With, like, tentacles, you know.'

'I don't think I do.' Sofia sounded nervous too.

But there was nothing there. The faint torchlight picked out the trail in the snow where something had dragged itself up onto the quay and along the roadway. And the deeper trail where something heavy had been pulled away.

'One of the soldiers?' Rose wondered. 'Jack couldn't get them on the radio.'

'If so, this man wouldn't have been alone,' Sofia pointed out.

'More than one, then. Maybe. Oh, I dunno, do I?' Rose protested. 'We should be getting back to the inn.'

Sofia was shining the torch along the trail. It was little more than an impression in the snow – no distinctive markings or footprints. Almost as if someone had rolled a snowball along.

'You say it was glowing?'

'Yeah.'

'But the snow hasn't melted. It's just been pushed aside and crushed.'

'So, it glows but it doesn't get hot. It was sort of bluish.'

'Not even warm. A few degrees above freezing is hot round here.' Sofia clicked her tongue, considering.

'That's why we need the generator working again, and quickly. Not for light so much as for heat. Though the institute has its own power supply if we get really desperate.'

'Jack'll sort it.'

'I hope so.' She shook her head. 'Too much,' she muttered. 'Too much, too soon. I'm not ready for this.'

'Who is?' Rose wondered.

Sofia seemed to gather herself and come to a decision. 'I want to look at the stone circle again, where we found poor Pavel's body.'

'What, now? In this fog?'

'It may be clearer up on the cliff. This is a sea mist. It won't be so thick higher up.'

'Even so.'

'I want to see if there's a similar trail up there. If we wait, the snow may obscure it.'

'It probably already has,' Rose pointed out. 'And if it hasn't, the soldiers have been trampling all round the place anyway.'

'You don't have to come,' Sofia said. She turned away. 'Go back to the inn and keep warm and safe there, if you like.'

Rose sighed. 'I'll come,' she said. 'You'll need someone to keep an eye out for angry blobs while you go poking about in the snow.'

A light came on about ten metres away. Its glow was dissipated by the fog. It flickered as if struggling to stay alight, then brightened slightly. It wasn't much, but it was a comfort. Rose could see that Sofia was smiling.

But the way the shadows and the mist obscured her face, for a moment she looked almost grotesque. Like a grinning skull. Then she moved and the moment was gone.

'Come on, then,' Sofia said.

They took one of the Jeeps from the institute. Minin drove, silent for most of the journey. It was more than just his concentrating on getting through the thickening mist.

'You got a problem with this?' the Doctor asked at last.

'Several.'

'I'll take the blame.'

'That's only one of the problems.'

'So what are the others?'

'Least of our problems will be digging through frozen ground. More of a problem is knowing where to dig.'

'Someone must know. We'll get directions.'

Minin wiped at the inside of the windscreen with the back of his hand. It made little difference. They had slowed almost to a walking pace.

'Fedor Vahlen will know. He digs the graves.'

'How's he do that?'

'He's a builder. Mainly repairing leaks and shoring up the older buildings. But he's got a digger.'

'That's OK, then.'

'Pavel was his son,' Minin said quietly.

'Oh. Right.' The Doctor thought about this. 'He should be glad to help, then.'

'Might be glad to help *you*. Vahlen and I… he doesn't like me.'

The Doctor turned to look at Minin. 'No one likes you,' he pointed out. Then he grinned. 'He'll like me, though. Everyone does. Guaranteed.'

Razul was rubbing his oily hands on a rag. 'There was a blockage in the main feed from the larger fuel tank. No wonder they had to keep topping it up. Should run for a couple of days now without needing any attention.'

'Fingers crossed,' Jack said. 'Well done.'

Sergeyev nodded, which seemed to be as close as he would come to congratulating his comrade.

'Right, let's get back to the institute and see who's checked in. We can't do much more till morning and this mist burns off.'

'If it does,' Sergeyev said glumly.

'Oh, you're a bundle of joy,' Jack told him.

Sergeyev scowled back.

Razul was smiling with amusement at their antagonism. But his smile froze as he tossed the oily rag into a corner. 'What was that?'

'What?' Jack asked.

'A sound. Just then. Listen.'

They all stood silently, listening. There was a scuffling, scraping sound from behind the generator, barely audible above its steady throb of power.

'It's nothing,' Sergeyev said. 'Just the machinery.'

'Or rats, maybe,' Jack suggested.

But Razul was not convinced. 'It sounded like

something outside, on the hull. Sliding across the outer shell of the submarine.'

Sergeyev gave a dismissive laugh. 'That's not possible,' he said. 'We are below the waterline.'

Vahlen took some persuading to leave his distraught wife and bring his digger to the graveyard. He glared at Minin, refusing point blank to talk to the man, and so the Doctor had to work his charm.

It only went so far before the Doctor lost his patience. 'Will you stop feeling so sorry for yourself and do something to help?' he demanded. 'Pavel's gone, and I'm sorry. But if you want to prevent anyone else having to suffer what you're going through, then I suggest you get off your backside and give us a hand.' He took a deep breath before continuing more quietly, 'There's something going on here that's wrong and dangerous. You know that. Everyone knows that. You ignore it or give it a mythical name because you think you can't stop it. But now that's got to change. It's time to make a stand. I can stop it. I *will* stop it. But I need your help. All right?'

The huge mechanical shovel bit into the frosted earth. It struggled to penetrate, the main body of the digger lifting off the ground. But then it cut through suddenly, the digger thumping back down as the shovel came up. Its arm swung round, dropping the dark earth onto the snowy ground. Tendrils of mist played round the scene, the exhaust from the digger thickening the air.

The older graves had proper headstones: all identical, all arranged evenly in neat rows – like soldiers on parade. But the more recent ones were marked by small wooden crosses and positioned haphazardly across the landscape.

'He was the last to die under similar circumstances,' Minin said as they watched the pile of earth growing. 'He's been in the ground for two years. You sure you want to do this, Doctor?'

'*Why* doesn't he like you?' the Doctor said in reply.

'As you said, no one likes me.'

'Yeah. But he *really* doesn't like you.'

The digger backed away. It drew level with Minin and the Doctor, and Vahlen leaned out of the cab. He spoke to the Doctor, ignoring Minin altogether.

'The casket's exposed now. You do what you have to. I'll get out of your way and fill it in again when you're done. I'd rather no one else knew about this.' The engine revved and the digger lurched forwards again. Then it stopped and Vahlen's head reappeared. 'You'll stop this? You'll make sure it doesn't ever happen again?'

The Doctor nodded. 'It might take a while. There may be some cost. But I'll stop it. Promise.'

Vahlen's head disappeared back into the cab, then the digger disappeared back into the mist.

'He used to work with a man called Chedakin,' Minin said.

They walked slowly across to the open grave. The Doctor had a spade over his shoulder. They looked down into the blackness.

'They were the best of friends. But Chedakin had a big mouth.'

'Careless talk costs lives,' the Doctor said.

'It cost him his, certainly.'

'Tell me.'

'They found him with a gun in his hand and a hole in the back of his head. Shot himself rather than be recalled to Moscow to explain his actions. That's the theory.'

'Suicide?'

Minin nodded.

'And Vahlen and the others blame you for that?' The Doctor jumped down into the grave. 'People are so short-sighted, aren't they,' he said. 'Right, let's get the lid off this coffin.'

The cold of the ground had helped preserve the wood and it took the combined efforts of the Doctor and Minin to lever the top from the plain wooden box that served as a coffin. Immediately, the stench from inside made them both gag.

'Well, we know he's still here,' the Doctor said.

Minin had a handkerchief clamped over his nose and mouth. 'Quick as you can,' he said, his voice muffled. 'Let's get this over with.'

They wrenched the lid away and looked inside.

The coffin was empty.

'He's gone! Then where's the smell coming from?' Minin said.

The Doctor was stooped down beside the coffin. He

had a test tube in one hand and a metal spatula from Catherine's lab in the other. 'He's still here, I'm afraid.' The Doctor was scooping something up from the bottom of the coffin and scraping it into the test tube. He stuck a rubber bung in the top and handed it to Minin. 'Hang on to this a mo.'

'What is it?'

'The clothes have rotted, probably an accelerated process. As with the body. Whatever did it drained the binding energy from everything, not just the bone and cartilage.' He tapped the test tube that Minin was now holding. 'That's what's left of the body.'

Minin stared at it in horrified disbelief. Inside was what looked like a lump of pale, colourless jelly. 'This was once a person?'

The Doctor pushed the lid back on the coffin and hauled himself out of the grave. 'Yep.'

'But how can someone end up like this?'

'Dunno. But –' he reached down and helped Minin climb out to join him – 'unless we find out soon, we might all end up the same way.' He took back the test tube and shoved it into his jacket pocket. 'Cheering thought, isn't it?' he said happily, waving through the mist for Vahlen to come and fill in the hole.

The sound of the generator was a gentle throbbing from behind them as they made their way back towards the main hatch. They had almost reached it when they heard the noise again. Slithering, sliding, scraping – from somewhere up ahead.

'I don't like this,' Razul whispered. He checked his Geiger counter, but the reading was the same as ever.

'It's ahead of us,' Sergeyev said.

'It does sound as if it's inside the boat now,' Jack agreed. 'Must be some machinery, or something loose shifting as the sub moves in the water.'

'It isn't moving in the water,' Sergeyev pointed out.

'Clever clogs,' Jack muttered. 'OK, then,' he said out loud, 'let's get out of here as quick as we can, agreed?'

The other two nodded. The ladder up into the conning tower was just ahead of them now, the whole metal world lit in blood red as only the emergency lighting seemed to work.

Razul reached the ladder first. He reached out for it, then pulled his hand away. 'It's slippery,' he said in a hushed voice.

'It's just rusty, that's all,' Sergeyev said. He reached out to check, then he too pulled his hand away. 'No, it's… it's as if it's been smeared with oil or grease or something.'

'Something cold,' Razul agreed. 'Icy. But sticky.'

'It's the only way out,' Jack said quietly. 'Do we debate what's happened or leg it?'

They were all three clustered round the ladder now. Sergeyev shone his torch at the rungs in front of them. 'Colourless,' he said. He moved the torch up, and they could now all see that something clear and viscous was coating the ladder. The beam of light reached the top of the ladder, illuminating the open hatch. And with a cry of surprise and fear, Sergeyev dropped the torch.

A glowing tendril, like pale seaweed, dropped down towards them, thrashing across the bottom of the ladder.

'Come on!' Jack led the way, running from the pale, glowing, gelatinous mass of the creature that was oozing down the ladder behind them.

'We should have headed back for the generator,' Razul gasped.

'There is no way out back there either,' Sergeyev said.

'No. But up here, we heard…' His voice tailed off.

They slowed to a halt. Their faces were pale even in the red of the lights. From behind them came the slithering sound as the creature dragged itself after them down the main corridor.

And from up ahead they could all hear the same sound. Not an echo, but another of the creatures.

'We're trapped between two of them,' Jack realised.

'It's cold, it's foggy and there's nothing here,' Rose announced. She was standing with her arms folded, close to one of the stones on the top of the cliff.

In front of her, Sofia was shining her torch slowly round the stone circle. The upright monoliths stood like soldiers waiting for orders – dark shapes wreathed with mist.

'Just a few minutes more,' Sofia said.

'Why? There's nothing.'

'I want to test a theory.'

'What theory?'

Sofia switched off the torch. Her pale face seemed to

glow in the suffused light. The tendrils of thin mist that wrapped themselves round her made the woman seem wraith-like, ghostly, as she stepped towards Rose.

'This creature must be part of it. So the systems are starting up on their own, without intervention.'

'What are you talking about?'

'I'm talking about a problem. My problem. It may all be coming to an end. I must know.'

Rose took a step back, away from the advancing woman. 'You're mental,' she muttered.

'And if the systems are activating themselves, then these stones will also be active all the time.'

'Active – what do you mean? What do they do?' Rose was seriously spooked now.

Sofia's face seemed as old as weathered rock as she took another step forwards. Then she suddenly lunged at Rose and grabbed her wrist, pulling her.

'Don't you know?' she hissed, her face close to Rose's. She seemed suddenly much older than Rose had thought. Then she turned Rose round, so she was facing the nearest stone – just a metre away.

'When they are active, when we turn them on, the stones drain the energy from anyone who touches them. They take it all, anything that can nourish and feed them. And leave just the empty skin.'

She shoved Rose away from her, holding her by the hair, forcing her face towards the stone.

SEVEN

There was a faint tingling sensation on her cheek, like static electricity. Rose pressed back, trying desperately not to let her face touch the stone. But inch by inch Sofia was forcing her head forwards, both hands tangled in Rose's hair as she pushed. Rose grabbed the woman's coat, tried to push her away, but there was no way she could stop her.

So she didn't try. She let her legs collapse beneath her, falling suddenly downwards rather than forwards. Her face was still perilously close to the smooth, cold stone, but as Rose fell Sofia cried out in alarm and surprise. Her hands were wrenched from Rose's head. Rose twisted as she dropped down, determined to stay away from the stone. At the same time she kept hold of Sofia's coat, trying to pull her down as well – downwards and forwards.

As Rose twisted, she saw Sofia crash into the stone. Crawling away through the churned-up snow, she heard Sofia's shriek of pain and fear – watched her stagger back, hands over her face as if burned.

Rose didn't wait to see what the damage was. She was struggling to her feet, slipping in the slush, stumbling forwards – towards the car.

She wrenched open the door and hurled herself inside. The door slammed shut, and a moment later Sofia was there, dragging it open again. Rose held on tight, let it open enough that she could slam it shut again, and pushed the handle across to lock it. Please don't let her have the key, she thought.

The key was still in the ignition. With a sob of relief, Rose turned it. The engine creaked and coughed but didn't start. She turned the key again.

And the windscreen cracked.

Sofia was kneeling on the bonnet of the car, hammering at the windscreen with the butt of her torch. Another crack with each blow. Another couple of goes and it would break. The woman's face was a snarl of rage as she raised the torch in both hands like a dagger, preparing to strike again.

Rose just stared. She was so old – recognisably Sofia Barinska, but twenty, thirty, maybe forty years older – her hair grey, face wrinkled and slack-skinned. Like Valeria had been. The teeth in her snarling mouth were black and crooked as the torch slammed down again.

The engine caught this time. Rose hadn't realised she was still turning the key. But she didn't hesitate. She slammed the gears into reverse and the car shot backwards – skidding and sliding across the icy ground. Unbalanced, Sofia fell back. But she managed to stay on the bonnet. The stones were behind the car, so Rose couldn't keep going in reverse.

First gear. The wheels skidded and slipped again as the car struggled to change direction. Rose could feel the front of the car digging into the earth. Wheel spin. No movement. The torch raised again.

Then one of the wheels got a grip and the car lurched sideways. Both wheels now and it shot forwards, towards the road. Sofia was knocked off balance and her aged face slapped into the windscreen, pressed hard against the surface – the lines on her skin like the cracks in the glass.

The car slewed sideways before skidding back on course for the narrow road lower down the hill. Still Sofia was on the bonnet, thumping at the glass with one hand while she clung on with the other. The torch bounced away. The largest crack got longer. The glass moved. The car reached the more certain surface of the road, and Rose hit the brakes.

The woman was a mass of flailing limbs and flapping coat as she was hurled off the bonnet. Rose pushed the accelerator, almost stalled as the clutch caught too abruptly. The car kangarooed forwards, got a grip, smacked into Sofia as the woman struggled to her feet and sent her flying sideways off the road.

Rose could see her through the side window, getting painfully to her feet and staggering away. Towards the squat grey block of the research institute – the one place Rose could go for help. Should she risk it? What were her options?

'The villagers won't believe me,' she said out loud as she drove along the track. 'Or if they do it'll be because they already know. Maybe they're all like her...' She could look for Jack, but he might be anywhere by now and she didn't fancy returning to the docks and the glowing blob creatures. She needed to find somewhere to hide, somewhere safe, somewhere with a phone or some means of contacting the Doctor at the institute and warning him.

Not the institute, then, and not the inn or the docks. She knew just the place.

Razul looked pale even in the red of the emergency lighting. 'We could hide in one of the cabins,' he whispered. 'Wait for it to go past.'

'Whatever it is,' Jack said quietly.

'If it does go past,' Sergeyev pointed out. 'It may be checking each room. We'd be trapped.'

'We're trapped now!' Razul hissed.

'Sounds as if it's on the bridge, or whatever you call it on a sub,' Jack said. He expected Razul to tell him the correct term, but the man was too far gone. He'd dropped the Geiger counter and was now shivering inside his uniform.

Towards the back of the boat there was a pronounced slithering sound. No doubt any longer that there were two of the things and they were trapped between them.

'I can see it,' Sergeyev whispered. He was pointing down the narrow corridor, towards the main hatch, the only escape.

A pale-blue blob was squeezing its way towards them, shimmering in the glow of the emergency lights. It all but filled the corridor, tendril-like tentacles probing ahead of it.

'Can it see?' Jack wondered. 'Or hear?'

'Who the hell cares?' Razul said. He pulled his rifle off his shoulder, took aim and fired at the hideous creature. The shots were incredibly loud in the confined space. They echoed and re-echoed round the metal corridor.

Tiny dark pinpricks appeared in the pale body of the creature. But as soon as they appeared, they were gone. The creature slithered forwards, unperturbed.

'Like shooting at jelly,' Jack said. 'Don't waste your ammo.'

'We can't get past it,' Sergeyev pointed out.

The creature had paused by an open bulkhead. A tentacle stretched out through the doorway, exploring inside.

'Think we could keep away from it?' Jack asked.

'I wouldn't like to try, Captain.'

'We must do something,' Razul protested. 'We can't just stay here, can we?'

Sergeyev was looking past them, the other way down the corridor. Jack saw him take in a deep breath and looked to see for himself.

There was another of the creatures dragging itself towards them from the other end of the corridor.

'You're right, we can't just stay here,' Jack said. 'Unfortunately there's no longer anywhere else to go.

Those things pretty much fill the width of the corridor. We'd never get past.'

'Then we go up,' Sergeyev said. 'Cling to the ceiling.'

'Up?' Razul's voice was trembling with nerves. 'Are you crazy?'

'There might be room,' Jack conceded. 'We can hold on to the pipes.'

'Wait up there for them to pass.'

'They'll see us,' Razul said.

'I think they're blind,' Jack told him.

'Think?'

'Look, do you have a better suggestion? Because if so now's not the time to keep it to yourself.'

'Too late,' Sergeyev said quietly. 'You think maybe they can hear, understand what we are saying?'

The creature from the back of the submarine had extended two of its tentacles upwards and outwards. It was feeling along the pipe-cluttered ceiling of the corridor. The pipes rattled and clanked as the creature felt its way along, probing into every possible hiding place.

'It was a good idea,' Jack said. 'So, we can't go up or along. If only we could...' He broke off. Sergeyev was staring back at him, realising at the same moment. 'Come on, quick!'

Razul watched for a moment, then, also suddenly understanding what they were up to, bent down to help.

Together they pulled up several of the metal plates that made up the floor. It took a moment as there were restraining pins at each side. But they just needed twisting to free the plates. They were heavy mesh, covering the crawl space beneath the floor. There looked to be just about enough space to lie flat underneath them. If they had time.

The creatures were inching their way forwards, tentacles thrashing ahead of them. One of the tentacles slapped down close to Razul, making him flinch.

'In, in quick,' Jack said as soon as the plates were free and clear.

Razul dropped down, and Sergeyev pushed a plate back down over him. There was no room to move, but it was too late now to worry about claustrophobia, Jack decided. He slid two more plates back into place over Sergeyev.

It was tricky easing himself into the space and pulling the final plates back. Jack had to hold the last plate up above him as he wriggled in, then lower it gently down over his face. It almost touched him and he had to turn his head sideways. The cold angles of the crawl space dug into him uncomfortably. A tentacle lashed out across the plate above him, then slid back, dragging wetly along the mesh like seaweed. It smelled like seaweed too – salty and damp and stale.

Then the creature was over him. The pale-blue glow of its body replacing the red of the lights. The creatures had almost reached each other. Would they realise where their prey had gone? Or would they go hunting elsewhere? When tentacle met tentacle rather than Jack and the others, what would they do?

The creature stopped. Directly above Jack, it stopped. He was trapped underneath a murderous alien blob with just a metal mesh between them. The weight of the thing was pressing its gelatinous body down into the holes in the floor plate. Glistening, wet blue flesh was extruding slowly but surely down towards Jack's face.

A scream echoed and rang through the submarine. Moments later, the sound was joined by the noise of the deck plates being ripped aside and tossed away as the creatures came after their prey.

The Doctor waved cheerily to the two soldiers on duty at the gates. If they were surprised to find the Doctor and Alex's Jeep followed by a digger, they didn't show it.

'He's with us,' the Doctor shouted as they pulled in to the compound.

Vahlen had asked if he could bury his son's body. It seemed a reasonable request, but neither the Doctor nor Alex could agree. The least they could do was allow him to pay his last respects. Alex tried to warn the man that it would not be a pleasant experience, but it was impossible to tell if Vahlen was even listening.

'Can't you make him look… decent?' Alex asked as the digger drew up noisily beside the Jeep.

'Death isn't decent,' the Doctor said.

'Something. A father shouldn't see his son like that.'

The Doctor thought of the emaciated, drained body and had to agree. 'Not sure what I can do,' he admitted. 'Maybe something.' He could at least put the scalpels and other surgical instruments away and drape a sheet over the poor boy.

'I'll keep Vahlen in my office for a few minutes. Give you time.'

The Doctor nodded. It was strange how concerned the man was, given that Vahlen obviously resented his mere presence. Strange, but commendable.

The Doctor did what he could, which was little enough. He consoled himself with the thought that Vahlen was a gravedigger. He knew that a body was a body was a body. He'd probably seen the other victims. Though nothing would prepare him for the sight of his son.

Minin appeared at the door to the laboratory after a few minutes. 'Ready?'

'As he'll ever be.'

Minin swallowed. He looked haunted, eyes hollow and tired. 'I gave him a drink. Least I could do.'

'Why d'you care?' the Doctor asked.

Minin shrugged. 'These are my people. This is my home. I care.' He left it at that.

The Doctor followed him back to his office. Vahlen was sitting at the desk, reading through a file of papers. From Minin's sharp intake of breath, the Doctor guessed this was not what Minin had expected or intended.

The old man looked up and his cheeks were stained with tears. 'They didn't let me see Vladimir's body,' he said. 'After he shot himself, after you drove him to suicide, or so we thought. They didn't let me see his body.' He waved a piece of paper; the edge of it was crumpled in his fist. 'Now I know why.'

Minin said nothing, but his face had drained of what little colour it had. He stepped aside as Vahlen pushed past and out into the corridor.

'You will take me to see my son,' Vahlen said to the Doctor. 'No more lies, no deceit.'

Gently, the Doctor took the paper from Vahlen. He smoothed it out, glanced at it, handed it back to Minin. Then he led the way to the laboratory.

In his office, the Doctor knew that Minin would be carefully replacing the paper in the file. The post-mortem report on Vladimir Chedakin. A report that pointed out that while the official verdict might be suicide, it was probably impossible for the man to have shot himself in the back of the head.

Rose parked the car round the back, out of sight. The front door was open and she went through into a typical village police station with a small waiting area and counter. Behind the counter was another door into the main part of the house. It was locked.

The telephone was dead. Maybe she needed to do something to get a line. She tried pressing 9, as on the phones at work. Still nothing. None of the numbers seemed to work and she gave up. She'd got her own mobile, of course, but had no idea what the code would be for this part of Russia – even if she could find a list of local numbers that she could read. Did the Russians use the same numbers – after all, their alphabet was different? Could she read Russian as well as understand it now?

Too many questions. The answers, if there were any, to explain Sofia's transformation and behaviour might be in her house. Rose hesitated only a moment at the door. She remembered the woman's snarling, murderous face pressed to the windscreen as she tried to break through and get Rose. She remembered her own face, perilously close to the stone. And she kicked the door open.

The house was sparsely furnished. The lights were naked bulbs. The carpet was threadbare. Everything was old and falling apart. She went rapidly from room to room, checking drawers of the desk, opening cupboards in the kitchen. Nothing at all. At least, nothing out of the ordinary.

Until the spare bedroom. There was no bed, no wardrobe or chest of drawers. Standing in the middle of the room, on the bare boards, was what looked like a dentist's chair. Except it had pipes and tubes running to a cylindrical metal device beside it. More thin pipes ran from this to the side of the room and down into the floor. Above the chair was a dome-shaped headpiece. Like a combination of headphones and a salon hairdryer.

Rose walked all round the chair. Then she went back downstairs to look for the pipes. They emerged in the corner of the kitchen. Rose followed them round the wall, through into the next room, out into the hallway. They disappeared finally into the wooden boards that enclosed the bottom of the staircase. And now she looked closely, Rose could see a door – no handle, no lock, but the blunt metal edges of the hinges and the way the cuts through the boards all lined up.

Except the door wouldn't budge. She broke a nail trying to lever the thing open. Cursing, she put her gloves back on.

Then she heard the door to the front office. Help? Or not? Rose ducked into the kitchen, looking for something to use to defend herself – anything. There was a serrated knife on the worktop, lying next to a scarred wooden board and a hunk of dry bread, but she knew she'd never use it. She hid behind the door, watching through the crack between the hinges as Sofia stepped into the hall.

Barinska was limping – almost dragging herself forwards. Why had she come back? She looked a wreck – a glimpse of her face made Rose almost cry out. Almost. If Barinska hadn't been wearing the same clothes, she could have been another woman – her grandmother. Or great-grandmother. Ancient, skin parched and lined, body shrunken and weak. Her breath a stentorian wheeze.

The old woman staggered as far as the hidden door under the stairs. 'Are you down there?' she croaked. 'Have you found it?'

Rose pressed back out of sight, knowing that Barinska was calling to her – knew she was here, somewhere.

Sofia Barinska leaned against the boards and the door

sprang open. She peered into the darkness beyond, as if considering. She looked close to collapse. After a moment, she pushed the door shut again and shuffled towards the stairs.

Rose pressed herself back, desperate not to be seen, though she doubted the woman could do her much harm now. She could hear the heavy breathing as the woman struggled up the stairs.

Eventually Rose crept into the hall. The stairs were clear. From above she could hear the sound of machinery – a building hum of power. Hardly daring to breathe, she went up the stairs, keeping to the side by the wall in the hope they wouldn't creak and betray her.

The noise was coming from the spare room. She risked a look round the door – just a peep. A glance and then she pulled back.

It was enough.

Sofia Barinska was sitting in the chair, the headpiece attached to her scalp. In that one glance, Rose could see all she needed to. She saw the form of the young woman trembling with satisfaction. Her youthful face set in a smile of triumph. Wisps of dark hair spilling out from the headpiece. The life force flowing through her and revitalising her. Making her young again.

As quickly as she dared, as quietly as she could, Rose went back downstairs. She ran to the hidden door and pressed urgently at the boards, where Sofia had leaned.

The door clicked open just as the hum of power from the upstairs room cut off. Rose went through, almost falling down the steep steps that led into the darkness below. She pulled the door closed behind her, cutting off the little light there was, and started slowly, carefully downwards.

The steps seemed to go on for ever. But at last she reached the bottom. She had her hand on the wall to steady herself, when her fingers bumped against something. She felt round it – a switch. Did she dare?

She pressed it, holding her breath, and the lights came on. They were hung at intervals along the tunnel roof – bare bulbs strung up in makeshift fashion, dusty and old. Some of them had blown and not been replaced. But it was enough. Rose could see now that she was in a tunnel hewn from the cold earth. The sides were shored up with planks of wood. The wood was old and bent with age. Some of the planks had rotted away. The floor was packed earth and the roof looked as if it had been hastily boarded over some time long ago.

All caution gone now that she could see where she was, and now that Sofia would know she was here if she came down and saw the lights, Rose ran. She ran for what seemed like ages. The tunnel was sloping gently downwards and she had no idea what direction it was going in. But it must lead somewhere. And the further and faster she got away from Sofia Barinska, the better. The sooner she found a way out into the open air – and escape – the better.

It ended eventually in what looked like the door of a bank vault – a round, heavy, metal door with a locking wheel and clamps across. Rose pulled the clamps back. They moved easily, which suggested the door was used often. The wheel swung just as smoothly.

Rose pulled the heavy door open, leaning back to let her full weight help drag it. Then she stepped through and looked around.

'You are kidding!' she whispered.

Jack was pressing himself down into the floor as hard as he could as the bluish flesh closed in on him. A sudden lurch of movement as the creature rolled forwards, the slivers of blue were pulled back through the mesh and moved on with it. As soon as it was past him, Jack heaved up the deck plate and pulled himself out. Ahead of him, the screaming stopped, abruptly, as if it had been switched off.

Jack was already pulling up the next plate as quickly and quietly as he could. He put his finger to his lips as Sergeyev looked up at him, eyes wide with fear. Sergeyev nodded, or as much as he could in the confined space. They hunted by sound – Razul had screamed and they had found him.

The creature was over the deck plate that covered Sergeyev's legs. Jack reached in and managed to get his hands under the man's arms. He pulled, dragging him clear – far enough for Sergeyev to be able to push himself up and out of the crawl space. They made their way quickly down the corridor away from the creatures.

'No hope for Razul and we're still trapped,' Sergeyev whispered. 'They're between us and the hatch.'

'Not if I draw them off,' Jack told him. 'You get into

one of the cabins. If they hear me, if they chase me, they won't stop to check. Let's hope,' he added quietly.

Sergeyev was shaking his head. 'I shall draw them off. I am a combat soldier, I expect to die. You Intelligence people – no backbone.' He smiled thinly. 'And having seen what it does, it's backbone it wants.'

'That's a good point,' Jack conceded. 'But I outrank you. Whether you like it or not, I'm in charge and you have your orders. Get in there.'

He pushed open the nearest cabin door and thrust Sergeyev inside. He didn't care about the noise it made. Didn't care that the creature ahead of him was slowly oozing back down the corridor. Slowly at first, but gathering speed. That was, after all, the point.

Sergeyev was at the door, protesting. But Jack waved him to silence.

'You complain and we're both dead. Get in there and shut the hell up!'

'Yes, sir.' Sergeyev hesitated, then unbuckled the holster round his waist. He folded the belt round the pistol and handed it to Jack. 'It might help.'

Jack nodded. They both knew it wouldn't. But the gesture was important, the trust it implied. 'Thanks. I'll give it back to you later.'

Again, they both knew he wouldn't. But Sergeyev nodded, saluted, stepped back from the door.

Jack ran, stamping his feet, hearing the sound of his rapid footsteps echoing metallically round the submarine. Hoping both the creatures would follow him.

And all too soon he was at the end of the corridor, in the wide, low room that filled the end of the sub. Alone and at the end of the road. 'What the hell are you doing, Jack?' he said out loud, looking round for any chance of escape. Any chance at all.

Well, if he was going to die he might as well put it off as long as possible. There was a heavy circular door into the room. It was rusted open, but by bracing himself against the bulkhead, Jack could just manage to move it. It swung closed, desperately slowly. A blue glow lipped over the door sill and into the room. Just a bit further. A tentacle stretched inwards, feeling round, probing the air above Jack's head. He shoved harder – a final effort.

The weight of the door broke through the rust and it swung suddenly smoothly on its hinges. It slammed shut with a clang and Jack spun the locking wheel. There was an unholy screeching of pain and anger from the other side of the door, barely muffled by the thick metal.

Behind him, a severed tentacle thrashed and careered about the room. It slammed into a rack of torpedoes. The rack collapsed, spilling the heavy cylinders across the floor. One of them trapped the end of the tentacle beneath it and the thing slapped spasmodically, slowly weakening while Jack ran to avoid the rolling weapons, hoping they didn't go off.

Finally, all was quiet and still. Jack sat down on one of the torpedoes and sighed. 'What a life,' he murmured.

He glanced over at the door. Watched it shudder and strain in its frame, as the creatures outside tried to force their way in.

EIGHT

Rose picked her way across the enormous room. It was like a cathedral made of rusted metal. Every surface was coated with a layer of dust or corrosion. Wires and shattered components littered the floor. The whole place was lit with a pale glow that seemed to emanate from the walls, floor and ceiling. Bizarrely, there was a clipboard lying on top of one of the control panels. It looked so ordinary it was completely out of place.

Her first thought was that it was another submarine – experimental perhaps. Open-plan. But the technology seemed so totally alien, and not just Russian-alien. Alien-alien. Blobby underwater aliens with flippers and snorkels? Get real.

She was almost at the main control chair, facing the largest of the instrument panels, before she realised there was someone sitting in it. Or rather, there had been. The body was slumped forwards, as if all the bones had shattered. It was almost mummified it was so old – desiccated and decaying.

There was another hatch, like the one she had entered through, on the far side of the ship. Beside it was an area taken up with long, low couches. Sleeping quarters perhaps, or a medical facility. There were sheets draped over the couches – thin and torn with age. Poking through the sheets Rose could see the remains of what looked like bodies – human bodies – beneath. She swallowed hard and ran for the hatch.

It opened as easily as the first. Only when she opened it did she worry about what might be outside.

In fact it was a cave – almost as big and impressive as the interior of the ship. But barnacled rock replaced corroded metal, and algae stood in for dust. Water was lapping at the edge of the shelf of rock she found herself on. The roof stretched away, gradually lowering to meet the water. The only way out of here was to swim.

The light was strange – a glow through the open hatch of the ship and the faint, dappled moonlight that shone through the clear, cold water. It was difficult to make out much detail, but obviously there was nothing of interest or use out here. Rose turned to go back inside the ship.

The sudden splash made her turn. Something was coming – rising up from the water, spluttering and coughing and lurching towards her. A shadow, a silhouette in the pale light. A shape looming up, arms outstretched, shaking uncontrollably.

She just stared in disbelief as the figure staggered up

onto the shelf of rock and sank to his knees.

'You scared the life out of me,' Rose said. 'What're you doing?'

'I think…' His teeth were chattering so much he could barely talk. Jack stared up at Rose, his face pale and his whole body shaking with the cold. 'I think I'm freezing to death,' he managed.

'You're not wrong,' she said, and hugged him tight.

The door was not quite closed. Sofia Barinska tapped thoughtfully on the wooden board beside the door. The girl Rose had been here – she'd left the car outside and broken the lock on the office door. What had she seen? What did she know?

If she had gone down the tunnel, then she would find the ship. She might not understand it, might not realise what it meant. But the Doctor surely would.

That was a risk she could not afford to take. Sofia opened the door and stepped into the darkness beyond.

He was still shivering, but Jack no longer seemed to think he was going to die. Rose managed to prise herself away, and sacrificed her coat to the cause. He sat huddled inside it on a spare chair inside the ship. At least he was up to taking an interest now.

'So who persuaded you to go swimming?' Rose wanted to know.

Jack pulled himself to his feet, stamping and pulling her coat tight about him. 'It was that or an appointment with the blob creatures,' he said.

'Oh yeah. I met one of them.'

'They had us trapped in the sub. Got Razul. I think Sergeyev made it. I hope.'

'What do you make of this, then?' Rose led him back to the area with the couches.

'Got myself stuck in the forward torpedo room, with no way out,' Jack was saying. 'Well, there was a way out but it was a bit drastic.'

'You had a tin-opener?'

'Sort of. I opened the torpedo tubes and flooded the place. Swam out through one of the tubes when the water stopped rushing in.'

'Sounds dangerous,' Rose conceded.

'I think it was. I don't think I'll ever be warm again in my life.'

'You might as well give me my coat back, then.'

'So what's all this?'

'Dunno. You tell me. You're the expert.'

'Spaceship. Old. Crashed. Source of the distress signal. What's under the sheets?'

'More bodies, like the pilot back there. Humanoid, I think, from the shape.' Rose pulled back the sheet on the nearest couch.

'You sure?' Jack said quietly.

Rose just stared. 'What the hell is that?'

The lecture theatre had not been used for years. But Colonel Levin had decided it was the best place to gather them all together. Several of the soldiers carried out boxes of papers and rubbish, another couple swept the floor.

One of the patrols had returned from the docks once they found they had lost radio contact. There was no sign of the others. Levin was sure they could take care of themselves and were waiting for the fog to clear. The Doctor was not so sure. He had expected to hear back from Rose and Jack by now. He was not worried exactly, but getting anxious.

Klebanov, in contrast to Levin's calm, was furious. The Doctor sat sideways in his chair, arms folded, stifling a yawn as the director let off another volley of invective.

'You have taken over my institute, filled it with your troops, encouraged Minin to indulge his bureaucratic fantasies, lost radio contact with your men, and now I discover you have invited some old workman from the village in for a drink!'

Levin raised an eyebrow. 'The radio blackout is a temporary phenomenon caused by the weather,' he said. 'And Minin has been cross-checking the supplies situation for me. We must know what equipment and facilities we have available to us. As for this old man...' He looked round, obviously expecting an explanation from one of his men.

The Doctor sighed and put his hand up. 'That was me,' he admitted. 'And it wasn't just some old man. It was Pavel Vahlen's father. He wanted to see his son's body, and I certainly wasn't about to tell him he couldn't because it might give some officious director an ulcer.' He met Klebanov's glare with a grin. 'Oh, and it's not the weather, by the way.'

'I'm sorry?'

'The problem with the radio. It's not the weather, it's the stones. In the circle. There's a vein of quartz-like material threaded through them.'

He looked at Catherine, who nodded in agreement.

'It seems to resonate, much like quartz,' she said. 'The Doctor thinks it's powerful enough to interfere with any transmissions.'

'Rubbish!' Klebanov announced. 'We'd have had trouble before now.'

'You have,' the Doctor told him. 'It's all in the logs. And strangely, as Alex here and I have found out, it tends to coincide with the deaths. Oh, yes,' he told Levin, 'they're not new either.' He stood up. 'Now, if we're all done, I've got things to do. And so's everyone else.'

'Oh, really?' Klebanov sneered.

'Oh, really,' the Doctor replied darkly. 'Levin needs to organise patrols. There's something nasty out there and we have to know what and where it is. Boris and Catherine need to analyse the weird rock sample I brought and see if they can find a way to stop this radio jamming. Alex and I have some more investigations to conclude, as well as finding Rose and Jack. If anyone can walk into trouble, they can. And you...' He shrugged. 'I dunno. I s'pose you must have something you can be getting on with.'

The meeting broke up with Levin telling his men he'd speak to them separately. The scientists, Minin and the Doctor took the hint and left quietly. Except Klebanov, who stamped out.

'So what's his problem?' the Doctor asked Alex Minin when they got back to his office.

'Klebanov? He likes to be in control. He's afraid his power is being taken away.'

'And what's his background? Where's he from?'

'I don't know.'

'Thought you had access to all the files.'

Alex nodded. 'So I do. But Klebanov doesn't have a file. He was here when I first arrived. Been here longer than anyone can recall. He's older than he looks.'

'Aren't we all,' the Doctor muttered.

'I can show you the records if you want. Whole room full of them.'

'Might be fun,' the Doctor agreed.

Alex laughed. 'I don't know about fun.' He led the way out of the office and down the corridor. 'I actually asked Klebanov for his file once. He got very angry. That was when he told everyone I'd been asking about the monkeys. You've heard about that, I expect?'

'Oh yeah. It was mentioned.'

'Wish I *hadn't* mentioned it now. Seemed important at the time.'

'Yeah?'

It was obviously something that still rankled. 'I mean,' he said, 'I know it's before I even came here, but the paperwork's all filed away and in order. The simians – that's how they're referred to – the simians were shipped out. They were signed for off the supply ship at the docks. Yet no one knows what happened to them.

They're obviously not here. But what would anyone want with half a dozen monkeys in a place like Novrosk?'

'Well, I've never seen anything like it,' Jack confessed. He had Rose's coat draped over his shoulders like a cape and he'd just about stopped shivering.

'Nor me.'

'I guessed that.'

'Thanks.'

They both stared down at the body on the couch. It was old and decaying, like the pilot. But it seemed a completely different species. In fact, it looked like more than one species. Parts of the body were almost human, or had been. But others seemed to have been grafted on. Or perhaps it was the other way round.

The result was a grotesque amalgam of human and animal. Dried, wrinkled dead skin gave way to matted fur. The taut, parched skin round the mouth suddenly extended into a dark, brittle snout. What should have been a foot had long, jointed toes curled into a tight grip like a fist.

'*Frankenstein* meets *Planet of the Apes*,' Rose said.

Jack was checking the other couches. All had similar creatures lying under the sheets. Six in all. 'What the hell happened here?' he wondered.

Before they could speculate, the hatch on the other side of the ship swung open. Sofia Barinska stepped into the ship. 'I thought I might find you here,' she said.

'It's OK. Just that policewoman,' Jack said.

Rose stepped in front of him, keeping him back. 'It's not OK,' she told him. 'She was old, dying. Then she sort of revitalised in a chair thing.'

Jack looked from Rose to Sofia, who was standing with her arms folded and watching them with amusement. 'Really?'

'Really. That was after she tried to kill me, of course.'

Sofia unfolded her arms and started across the ship towards them. 'I shall make a better job of it this time,' she said.

All trace of tiredness or age had gone as she leaped at them. Rose recognised the knife from the kitchen as it swung towards her.

Her cry was lost in the sound of the gunshot. The knife went flying. Sofia was clutching her bloody hand. Jack was standing with the pistol braced in both hands. Rose's coat had fallen from his shoulders and lay in a heap on the floor.

The second shot caught Sofia in the chest, driving her backwards and knocking her off her feet.

Rose grabbed her coat. 'Come on.'

But Sofia was struggling slowly to her feet, chest a mess of red, hands slick and wet as they scrabbled for a hold on the floor to push herself up.

Another shot. Then Jack was grabbing Rose's hand and pulling her the other way – back towards the medical area.

'No, no,' she protested. 'We can get out down the tunnel.'

But Jack wasn't listening. He dragged her through the

hatch and slammed it shut behind them.

'She's dead,' Rose protested.

'Sure? Because I'm not hanging around to check.' He was spinning the locking wheel on the outside of the hatch. 'There has to be a way to keep this closed.'

'Why does there?'

'Because we need it.'

'And what now, then, Mastermind? I thought you'd had enough of swimming.'

'I have.' He was smiling. 'We go up the steps.'

'You what?' Rose turned to see where Jack was pointing. 'Oh, right.'

A flight of steps had been cut into the rock beside where the ship was embedded in the cave. She hadn't seen that before, hidden as they were in the shadows. But then she'd been more concerned with stopping Jack from freezing to death.

'I can guess where they go,' he was saying as he led the way.

Rose followed, pulling on her coat as she went. 'Good. Because I've no idea where I am.'

There was a door at the top. An ordinary door of the sort that might lead into an office. It opened a couple of inches, then stopped. Jack put his shoulder to it and Rose could hear something heavy shifting on the other side. She looked through the widening gap and saw a mass of cardboard boxes piled up against the door.

The door jammed. Rose helped Jack shove, but it wouldn't open any further. 'We're never getting through there,' she said.

As she spoke, a pair of hands appeared the other side of the door and started lifting the boxes away.

'Friend or foe?' Rose whispered.

'We'll soon find out.'

The door was swinging open. Beyond it was a small room. The floor was stacked high with the cardboard boxes. Papers spilled across the floor. A rack of metal shelves dominated the opposite wall, more boxes crammed into it.

And in the middle of it all stood a tall man with thinning, greying hair wearing a crumpled suit. Beside him was the Doctor.

'Oh, thank God, it's you,' Rose said. 'Hey, you'll never guess what we've found.'

The Doctor was peering past them, although all he could possibly see was a rock wall and the steps leading down into the cave. 'So that must be the secret way down to the old spaceship, right?' he said. He grinned, hugged Rose to him with one hand and slapped Jack on the back with the other. 'Fantastic!'

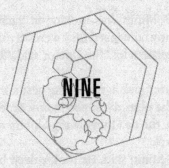

NINE

Alex Minin was looking bewildered. 'I never knew that door was there,' he said.

'Hidden,' the Doctor replied. 'Someone deliberately stacked all these boxes in front of it.'

'And what's this about a spaceship?' Minin laughed nervously, as if to show he knew they were joking really.

'Yeah. Spaceship,' the Doctor told him. 'You know.' He demonstrated by flattening his hand into a spaceship shape and flying it through the air between them. He made spaceship noises.

'I don't think I do actually,' Minin said weakly.

'Sure you do. You must get some version of *Star Trek*, even out here.'

'The one with Mr Spocksky,' Rose added helpfully.

'A spaceship?' Minin said.

'A spaceship,' Jack confirmed. 'And a homicidal mad policewoman killer-zombie as well. No extra charge.'

'Make that knife-wielding homicidal mad policewoman killer-zombie,' Rose reminded him.

'Barinska?' Minin was looking at each of them in turn, evidently convinced they were all mad.

'That'd explain a lot,' the Doctor said. 'Right, let's get going.'

'Good move,' Jack agreed. 'I suggest a three-pronged initiative. The objectives, not in any order of priority, are the ship, the deadly glowing blobby creatures and the stone circle.'

'Hold on,' Minin said. He took a deep breath. 'What deadly glowing blobby creatures?'

'They'll be the remotes,' the Doctor said, as if this was obvious.

'Remotes?' Rose echoed.

The Doctor nodded. 'Shouldn't be a problem.'

'They're killing people,' she pointed out.

'So, *shouldn't* be a problem, but they are.' The Doctor sucked in his cheeks and folded his arms. 'Someone's been messing about.' He turned to look at Minin. 'Monkey business,' he said quietly.

'Oh yeah, that's something else,' Rose put in. 'You see, there's these bodies.'

The Doctor stopped her, pressing his finger to her lips. 'First things first. Alex – go and find the colonel. Tell him his missing men have probably been blobbed by now and he's to forget them. Then bring him down to the ship.'

'He'll never believe there's a spaceship down there,' Minin said. '*I* don't believe there's a spaceship down there.'

'He will when he sees it,' Jack told him.

'It crashed here centuries ago. Maybe millennia,' the Doctor said. 'Crew's probably dead.'

'Yep,' Jack said.

'And it landed at the base of the cliff. Maybe even in the sea. Then over time the land has moved, and now it's buried under the cliff, close to this institute. Through that door.'

'But hang on…' Minin pointed to the open door. 'Why would anyone build a secret door leading down to a buried spaceship no one knows is there?'

'That's a really good question,' the Doctor agreed. 'You get Colonel Levin and we'll try to get some answers.'

On the way down to the ship, Jack and Rose told the Doctor their stories. He asked few questions and made few comments. But when Jack described the creatures that had cornered him and the soldiers in the submarine he exclaimed, 'Blue? Don't they know that's such a cliché?'

'Maybe where you're from. They're usually green here,' Rose said. 'I don't care what colour danger is. It's still… well, dangerous.'

'Yeah, but I mean – dangerous and boring?' the Doctor sneered. 'Do me a favour. If you're going to have your life threatened, it might as well be fun.'

'Trip of a lifetime,' Rose muttered.

The hatch was still closed. Jack put his hand on the Doctor's shoulder as the Doctor turned the locking wheel.

'You sure you want to go in there?'

'Yep.'

'Mrs Knife-Attack might be waiting. I shot her a few times, but she didn't seem as impressed as she should have been.'

'Probably not. She's been dosed up on mutagenic revivification enhancement energy for a while.'

Rose looked at Jack. 'What's he on about?'

'MRE,' Jack said. 'Like, life force.'

'Then why not say "life force"?' Rose said.

'Look, I didn't write the manual,' the Doctor protested. The hatch swung open. 'Anyway, she's probably legged it back to her house to recharge by now.'

'Let's hope,' Rose said. 'So you know all about it, then? Recognise the ship?'

'General type,' the Doctor admitted. 'Can't say for certain, but the technology's pretty standard for the Arcane Collegiate.'

'Never heard of it,' Jack admitted.

'It's pretty… esoteric.' The Doctor was examining one of the mutated, fused bodies. He drew the sheet back over it sadly. 'Like I said. Monkey business. Someone's been mucking about with the receptors.'

Rose was getting impatient. 'Look, will you just tell us what is going on here? Those of us who don't speak Spaceman would like an explanation.'

'And those of us who do wouldn't object,' Jack added.

'OK.' The Doctor wandered across to what seemed to be the main control area. He tipped the remains of the pilot out of its seat and flopped down in its place.

Rose gaped. 'Oh, gross.'

'He's dead, isn't he?'

The Doctor waved at them to make themselves comfortable. Rose sat on the floor, while Jack leaned against an instrument panel.

'He was probably killed in the crash, or at least his body was,' the Doctor said. 'Not much sign of damage, so the auto-repair fixed the ship up. But no pilot, so it's stuck. Thinks it's missed something, probably – some component that still needs attention. Or it needs new parts. So the ship sends out a signal. Come and help, please. Run out of fuel or need a new carburettor or whatever.'

'And who does it send this message to?'

'No one. Everyone. Just beams it out into space. Probably quite a strong signal to begin with. We caught the tail end – as the power runs down, it weakens.'

'Then what?' Rose asked.

'It gets more power,' Jack said.

He was nodding as if things were becoming clear to him. They were clear as mud to Rose.

'That's right. It doesn't need much, not till it gets ready for flight. Just enough to keep the systems up and running, ticking over, and to keep the message going. Now it can absorb energy from the environment. Heat, light, power of the wind, anything.'

'Life force,' Rose said quietly.

The Doctor nodded. 'That too. But not just that. Not in theory. Anyway, it sticks up its antennae and starts to draw the power.'

'Antennae?'

'The stones,' Jack told her. 'That's right, isn't it, Doctor? We're right under the stones here.'

'This ship is made of *stone*?' Rose asked. She looked round at the instrument panels – what she had assumed was brittle plastic could be stone, she realised. Thin, sculpted, shaped...

'Sort of, yeah. Like I said, the stones are antennae, prodded up through the ground till they reach daylight,' the Doctor said. 'Absorbing power. Same substance as the remotes, the blobs. Only solidified to withstand the elements and the test of time. It's all based on some pseudo-silicate material.'

'And then anyone who touches the stones,' Rose said, 'they'd be, like, drained of life force.'

'I doubt that was the original intention. It just needs a steady stream, a trickle of energy. But someone's tampered with the systems. It's designed to accept any type, any strain, of energy. Maybe it has a safety feature that excludes the life force from intelligent beings – even humans,' he added with a grin.

'Oh, ta,' Rose told him.

'But now someone's changed things round. They've adapted them so they deviate from the original plans and just take one defined strain of energy – life force. And probably just the life force of human beings. Certainly it didn't like mine when I activated a bit of stone, though it took Catherine's no problem. So it's no longer working to design. Now it's only interested in the deviant strain.'

'You mean us.'

'I mean you.'

'Hang on, what do you mean by "activated"?' Rose asked.

'They don't do it all the time. Just when the ship needs some power. It's automatic unless there's some other need for the power. Then someone, the pilot usually, switches it on.'

'Except someone else has changed things, so now they can activate the probes and draw life force whenever they need it,' Jack said.

'No prizes for guessing who,' Rose realised.

'But it's going crazy now,' Jack said. 'There's attack of the blob monsters out there, and the stones are probably getting thirstier all the time. Is that all down to Mrs Knife-Killer Barinska going bananas?'

'Doubt it,' the Doctor said. 'That's all someone else's fault.'

Jack shook his head. 'Wait till I get my hands on them. Have you ever crawled through a torpedo tube in the dark with water pouring in?' He hesitated. 'OK, *you* probably have. So whose fault is it?'

The Doctor was examining his fingernails. 'Actually,' he said, looking up at Jack, 'it's yours.'

'What?!'

The Doctor shrugged and went back to looking at his nails. 'You answered the message. You told the ship we were coming to get it. So now it's preparing to be rescued, getting ready to leave.'

'And it needs more power,' Rose said. 'Is that it?'

'Yep. The stones are no longer drawing enough for it, especially as up till now they've only got power when they're switched on here and someone touches them.'

'Switched on?'

'Yeah, there's a manual switch wired in rather crudely on that panel.' He nodded at where Jack was leaning. 'Don't shuffle your bum too much or you might turn them on again.'

'And these blob creatures?'

'Remote probes. Energy sources don't come to it, so it goes looking for them. They drain the energy and beam it back. The radio interference is a side effect as the ether fills with life-force transmissions.'

Rose thought about all this. 'Thanks, Jack,' she said at last. 'Good one.'

Jack sighed. 'So, at the risk of sounding as if I'm changing the subject, why did Barinska adapt the systems and what's she need the energy for?'

Rose was wondering that too. She thought about Barinska's face – lined and aged almost beyond recognition… 'She's old, isn't she? She needs the life force to stay young.'

'Seems likely. That's why only human energy would do. I doubt she's the only one either. There's been a lot of mucking about with these systems. Lots of trial and error to get to this point. Though a lot of it is informed guesswork. I think they've had help, even though they may not realise it.'

'I wonder how old she really is,' Jack said.

'She looked ancient,' Rose told him. 'So, come on

then. What happens now?'

'The ship keeps searching for energy. It'll store all it can until take-off.'

'Except it isn't gonna take off,' Jack pointed out. 'The pilot's dead, no help is coming. Unless, we…' He pushed himself away from the panel and turned to examine it.

'No good,' the Doctor told him. 'No way this thing can fly now. Too much damage and adaptation.'

'So, what – it just keeps looking for energy?' Rose asked. 'For people to kill?'

'Yep.'

'For how long?'

'Till it leaves.'

Rose stared at him. 'But… that's for ever.'

'Yep. Unless we can find a way to drain it right down, even the emergency reserves. Then the systems will stop.'

'How do we do that?' Jack was ready at the control panel.

'Dunno. Dunno if it can even be done until I take a proper look.'

'Oh, you're a real help in a crisis,' Rose told him.

'So what happens now?' Jack asked.

The Doctor opened his mouth to reply. But it was not him who answered.

'Now, you die,' a voice said.

It came from behind the panel where Jack was. He swung round in surprise. Just as Sofia Barinska's bloodstained figure rose up from behind it.

'We shall get all the energy we need,' she said. 'For ever.'

The knife flashed as it caught the light, stabbing down towards Jack.

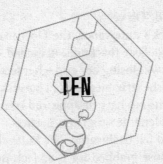

TEN

The Doctor did not seem at all fazed by the fact the woman was forcing a knife down at Jack's throat.

'How old are you?' He sounded as if he was telling off a schoolkid. 'I mean, really – how old?'

He was watching with interest as, to Jack's relief, Rose ran to help. The two of them were holding the woman's hands now – forcing the blade upwards. But Barinska was incredibly strong, and she had her full weight behind the knife, trying to force it back down.

'Levin said he thought he recognised you and you told him that was your mother. But it wasn't, was it?'

The Doctor stood up as he spoke and wandered casually over to watch the struggle. 'I think you were here before that, weren't you? Maybe before the navy came. Before the scientists. One of the original whaling community, maybe.'

'Some help here would be nice,' Jack gasped.

'You didn't work it out all by yourself, did you?' the Doctor was saying. Then he seemed to realise what

Jack had said. 'Oh yeah.'

But to Jack's annoyance, the Doctor did not try to help them deflect the knife. It inched closer to him again. Rose was losing her grip – her feet sliding across the floor as she struggled to hold Barinska's wrists. The Doctor seemed to have disappeared completely.

Then suddenly it was over. Barinska gave a cry of surprise and fell backwards. The knife clattered to the floor and Rose grabbed for it as Jack pushed himself away from the control panel.

'What happened?' Jack asked.

The Doctor's voice came from the other side of the panel. 'I kicked her feet away.' His delighted face appeared above the panel and he waved. 'Come and see.'

Barinska was lying face down on the ground. The Doctor had his foot on her back, as if she was a hunting trophy. The woman was lying completely still, but the Doctor kept his foot firmly planted in position.

'You didn't answer my questions,' he told her. 'But I bet you can feel it, can't you? The lingering presence in your mind of the dead pilot's own life force. His mental energy – guiding you, instinctively, to repair the systems. To survive long enough to get the ship working again.'

Barinska did not move.

'You mean he ain't dead at all?' Rose said.

'Oh, he's dead as a dodo. Just his mind, or part of it, lives on in the systems. Symbiosis. The pilot is one with the machine – his body may die but his mind lingers, like I said. Reaching out like the message. And what,' he asked Barinska, 'you found the ship and it talked to you, in your head, is that it?'

'That's how she was able to adapt the systems,' Jack realised.

'Yeah. Her and her mates, whoever they are. They think they want to live for ever. But actually it's the ship and the pilot that want them to live for ever. Or until the repairs are finished. Irony is, keeping its little helpers alive means the ship's crippled for good.' He rolled Barinska with his foot. 'I know you're not unconscious,' he told her. 'So who else is in on this, eh? Who else still thinks their life is their own?'

The reply was an angry, guttural snarl. Barinska rolled suddenly over and leaped to her feet. Jack made a grab at her, but she was too quick – darting past and heading quickly for the hatchway leading out into the cave.

The door opened before she got there. Colonel Levin was framed in the doorway, his pistol drawn. He stared in surprise at the woman rushing towards him.

'Stop her, Colonel,' Jack shouted.

Several of Levin's men had entered behind him. They levelled their assault rifles as Levin ordered, 'Halt!'

But Barinska kept coming.

Levin hesitated. 'Halt, or I fire.'

Barinska was almost on them now.

'Fire!' Jack shouted.

Perhaps out of fright, perhaps realising the danger, perhaps instinctively obeying the order, the nearest soldier fired.

The bullets slammed into Barinska, knocking her backwards. She fell on her back with a groan.

Levin raised his hand to stop the firing. All the soldiers moved slowly towards the figure on the ground.

'I'd be careful,' the Doctor cautioned.

Even as he said it, Barinska heaved herself off the floor and ran full pelt at the troops. The soldier who had shot her was standing gaping at the wounds he had inflicted. Then Levin fired. A moment later the others fired too.

All except the soldier who had shot first. It was too late for him. Barinska's arm swept round viciously, catching him in the neck. He stumbled and fell, and as he crashed to the floor Barinska's boot caught him under the chin, snapping his head back with an audible crack. She grabbed his rifle as he fell, turned, levelled it.

The woman was driven back by the volley of bullets from the soldiers, so most of her own shots went wide. But one of the soldiers caught a round in the shoulder. Another was knocked backwards as several bullets smacked into his chest.

Barinska was staggering under the automatic fire. She still clutched the rifle but was unable to bring it to bear. She managed to turn, running back across the ship towards the Doctor, Jack and Rose.

Jack and Rose dived to the floor. The Doctor, however, was still out in the open. Bullets thudded into the floor as Barinska managed to fire. Dust kicked up at the Doctor's feet. He didn't hesitate. He turned and ran.

Jack twisted, enough to see the Doctor make it through the hatch on the opposite side of the control deck. He disappeared rapidly up the tunnel the other side.

Then Barinska herself came into view – running after the Doctor, rifle at the ready. Her clothes were stained red and there were dark scorch-ringed holes across her chest. One bullet had all but taken off her jaw, leaving the skin ripped so that the lower half of her face was smiling like a skull. It did not seem to have slowed her down at all.

Levin and the soldiers reached the hatch just moments after Barinska. But it was moments too late. The heavy metal door had swung shut behind her. Now it was locked.

'There must be a way to open it from in here,' Levin said.

Jack got to his feet and dusted himself down. He looked round at the rewired panels. Several of them were smoking from bullet impacts. 'You want to guess which control to use?' Jack asked.

'Where does that tunnel lead?' Levin snapped.

'To Barinska's house,' Rose told him.

'You know the way?'

She nodded.

'Show us.' Levin pointed to two of the soldiers. 'You two, medical detail. Do what you can for the wounded.'

The Doctor's plan, such as it was, was to escape from Barinska without being shot. If he could stay ahead he might get a chance to look at the equipment she had in her house – which, according to Rose's story, was where this tunnel led. From that he might be able to come up with an idea of how to cut off her supply of energy. The problem with this was of course that he could hear her running after him, and every now and again a bullet whined past his head or smacked into the floor at his feet to remind him that Barinska had something of an advantage.

Maybe he'd skip the tour of her house and just leg it. He could meet Rose and Jack back at the institute later and decide how to deal with the spaceship. And the remote probes. And Barinska. And he had noticed she said 'we' when describing her ambition to live for ever, so presumably she had friends with a similar investment in keeping the ship intact, though he had guessed that from the monkeys...

'Who wants to live for ever?' the Doctor muttered as he ran. 'Just today would be a start.' Another bullet flew past him, and he wondered how many there were in the clip. And how many she had used. And whether there was another clip attached to the gun. Not a very helpful line of enquiry, he decided.

He could still hear Barinska behind him as he started up the steps. Her breath was ragged and hoarse, but she did not seem to have been slowed down by her wounds. Rapid repair, inherited from the ship's systems maybe. Something else he could wonder about later.

The Doctor slammed the door at the top of the steps behind him. There did not seem to be any way to lock it and he couldn't see anything to use to jam it shut quickly enough. So he ran.

Forget the equipment upstairs – come back for that later. The air was ice cold in the Doctor's mouth, throat and lungs as he emerged from Barinska's house and set off down the road. Anywhere to hide? Not really – she was too close. As in the house, she'd see if he tried to duck in anywhere. Just keep going, hope to extend his lead or that she would tire.

Along the road. Towards the harbour – rusting cranes and abandoned loading gear thrusting up out of the snow – black against the grey night sky. Then mist – as he approached the sea, the mist was rolling in. That might help, might obscure him for long enough.

A junction at the end of the quay – choices, decisions. He went left, and realised almost at once it was a mistake. He was on the quay now, a section jutting out into the bay. A jetty. No way off, except by diving into the water. And even that wouldn't work, he saw, as he glanced over the side. The sea was frozen to ice. He would be exposed on a white carpet – a perfect target even in the mist.

Bullets cracked across the roadway. He could almost hear her snarls of rage. His lungs were bursting, while the icy air was making his cheeks sting and his ears burn. 'Next time,' he gasped, 'smaller ears. Definitely.'

Dark shapes ahead of him as he neared the end of the jetty. A submarine, listing to one side. Not hopeful – his weight might sink it. Probably it was half flooded anyway. A death trap, he thought ruefully, as another volley of bullets kicked up puffs of snow around him.

A stark silhouette beside the sub. Crates and metal drums. Somewhere to hide, or at least take cover. Maybe. More shots as the Doctor leaped, scrambled over a crate, dived behind the nearest of the drums. He could see now, he realised. Everything was lit in a dull blue glow. And with bullets ricocheting round him, the Doctor saw that he was crouching behind an oil drum.

'Not good,' he said aloud. But perhaps the drum was empty. He pushed at it experimentally. It didn't budge. 'Not good at all.'

And stacked alongside were a dozen more drums. Diesel, probably. Waiting never to be used to refuel the submarine beside him. 'Oil. Gunfire. Torpedoes and missiles… Definitely not good.'

He looked round for something that might help. Anything. A cautious glance over the top of the drums revealed Sofia Barinska walking slowly down the jetty, gun levelled and ready. Her face was a mixture of blood red and pale blue. Where was that light coming from?

In fact, it seemed to be getting brighter. Coming, it seemed, from the end of the jetty behind him.

From the glutinous, hideous creature that was hauling itself up onto the end of the roadway and slithering slowly towards where the Doctor was crouching. A tentacle lashed out, slapping across the oil drum beside him. It pulled back, dragging the drum over onto its side. The drum scraped and boomed as it fell, started to roll.

Alerted by the sound, Barinska opened fire.

Another tentacle shot out, landing beside the Doctor. Then another. The creature was moving more quickly now, straight towards the Doctor, quivering, shimmering, glowing… More tentacles.

Another burst of gunfire. A ragged line of holes punched into the rolling drum and liquid spilled darkly into the snow.

A tentacle smacked into the Doctor's side, curled, grabbed, wrapped itself round him and started to pull him back. He could feel himself weakening in its grasp.

More shots.

The roar of ignition as the fuel oil caught.

Fire running from the rolling drum, back towards the Doctor and the other oil drums.

A tentacle crashing into the middle of the stack, sending drums flying, tumbling, rolling into the flames.

Then the explosions. Oil spilling, igniting, burning. Lighting up the misty night. A wave of fire crashing towards the Doctor as he struggled to break free.

ELEVEN

A dark figure emerged from the fiery mist: Sofia Barinska, looking from side to side, the gun ready. The Doctor was tearing desperately at the tentacle round his waist, trying to prise it away. Without success.

But he was no longer weakening. As in the lab earlier, he could feel the strength coming back as the creature – or rather the ship's systems – decided it wasn't interested in his life force. And despite the situation, the Doctor could not help noticing that the creature had stopped its advance. Even before it assessed his life force it had slowed and stopped. He didn't have time to wonder why – Barinska had seen him.

She gave a shout of triumph that was almost lost in the roar of the flames around them. The gun swung up.

The tentacles unwound rapidly from the Doctor, leaving him gasping in the hot smoky air. Then the creature lashed out sideways, sensing a better source of energy. Tentacles flew straight at Barinska.

The gun was swept aside as she pulled the trigger, the shots firing into the air and lost in the black smoke that blotted out all light except for the fire. A second tentacle thrashed after the first. Barinska's screams were gradually getting fainter. Her arms reached out towards the Doctor, her eyes were wide, begging for help.

He could only watch as she was dragged along the quay, leaving a black trail in the snow behind her. The creature was backing away, keeping well clear of the fire. The Doctor stood watching – the flames behind him, the smoke swirling round him like fog. Watching as Sofia Barinska's face cracked and crumpled and withered, and she disappeared into the darkness.

Rose was outside the inn when the quay exploded, leading the soldiers from Barinska's house back towards the docks. Even through the thickening sea mist she could see the ball of flame erupting into the air. She felt the heat on her face and skidded to a halt. Jack was beside her, Levin and three of the soldiers close behind.

The door of the inn opened and several people ran out to see what was happening.

'Down by the dry dock,' one of them said. 'Poor old Nikolai kept spare fuel oil down there. Didn't want it too close to the *Rykov*.'

'The Doctor?' Levin said, waving his men forwards.

'Who else would it be?' Rose told him. 'Come on.'

It looked as if the whole of the roadway was on fire as

they approached. The street lights were still on, struggling to make an impression through the smoke and fog. The end of the quay was burning. And out of it walked a lone figure – black against the red. The Doctor.

'Singed my jumper,' he complained as he reached them. 'Look at that.'

Rose pulled him into a hug.

'And now it's getting crumpled.' He was grinning as he said it.

'Where's the woman?' Levin asked. 'Where's Barinska?'

The soldiers were taking up position along the quay, aiming their assault rifles into the ball of fire, waiting to see if anyone else emerged from the inferno.

'She won't be joining us,' the Doctor said. He was already walking back along the quay, one arm round Rose.

'You don't believe in doing things quietly, do you, Doctor?' Levin said. 'Now perhaps you can tell us what the hell is going on here.'

'Need to know, Colonel,' Jack said.

'He does need to know,' Rose pointed out.

'Does he? Oh, right.' Jack nodded. 'The inn?'

'That's hardly a secure environment,' Levin said.

'True,' Jack told him. 'But you're going to need a drink.'

'Probably several,' the Doctor called back to them. 'Let's hope the company's… safe.'

* * *

Levin and his men listened intently to the Doctor's story. There was silence when he finished. Most of the villagers who were still up drinking had gathered round to listen as well. They looked more sober now than they had ten minutes before, Rose thought.

'D'you believe me?' the Doctor asked.

'I don't have a better explanation,' Levin conceded. 'Call it a working hypothesis until I do.'

'Fair enough,' Rose said.

'So what do you propose we do? We could mine this spaceship – blow it to bits.'

Jack shook his head. 'You'd be releasing a pent-up store of colossal energy that could do untold damage.' He smiled thinly. 'Says that in the handbook.'

'Yeah,' the Doctor agreed, 'and it wouldn't stop the remotes. They'd just keep gathering energy to try to provide sufficient power for the ship to rebuild itself.'

Any further discussion on the subject was cut abruptly short by a commotion on the other side of the inn. Someone was shouting and people were rushing towards the door.

Rose looked across in time to see old Georgi stumble in. He was holding a white stick – waving it in front of him as he staggered across to the bar. Several of the locals ran to help him.

'They're coming!' Georgi was shouting. 'I can see them. See them in my mind. Glowing, hunting, killing... Coming for us.' His sightless eyes were wide and blank, staring up at the men helping him to a seat.

'Who's that?' Jack asked.

'It's Georgi,' Rose told him. 'He saw that bloke's death – the one who kept the generator running. Georgi saw it happen. Like, in his mind's eye.'

'Oh, sure,' Jack said.

'He did!'

'It's possible,' the Doctor said quietly.

'You're not serious?' Levin countered.

'The ship communicates somehow with the remotes. That might be on a psychic wavelength. If this guy's alpha waves are operating on a similar frequency he might pick up on the link to the ship. He might actually see what the remotes are sending back.'

'So can we tell what they're up to?' Rose wondered, watching as someone handed Georgi a drink and the old man swigged it back in one.

'They're on their way,' he gasped. 'We have to get away from here – now!'

'Early warning system,' Jack said quietly. 'I guess it's possible.'

The Doctor was nodding enthusiastically. 'And if he can tap into the wavelength he might even be able to send the remotes different instructions. He might be able to block the ship's orders, maybe even control the remotes himself.'

'He doesn't look as if he's really up for it,' Rose told them. 'He's old, he's frightened, and if he drinks much more he won't be able to stand up.'

The Doctor considered. 'I'll need some time.'

Levin had been listening with interest. 'You really think this might work?' he asked.

'If he's already attuned,' the Doctor said slowly, 'we're halfway there. I can help him focus his thoughts, but we'll need somewhere quiet where he can concentrate.'

'But how much time do we have?' Jack asked.

A window close to the door exploded in a shower of glass. A glowing blue tentacle whipped across the room, sending a table crashing sideways and knocking chairs over. A second tentacle smashed through another window. Then a third.

'Not much,' the Doctor said.

The door burst open. A wall of throbbing blue pulsed in the opening. The wooden frame was splintering as the creature forced its way inside. Tentacles slashed across the room – glasses, tables, people went flying.

One of the men helping Georgi was side-swiped by a thrashing tentacle. It curled and clutched, grabbing him, rolling round him. The man's face crumbled as he screamed and fell.

'Back – everyone away from the door,' Levin was shouting.

His men had instinctively taken up defensive positions, their weapons aimed at the blue mass in the doorway. One of them opened fire, and then another. Soon they were all shooting. Small black holes scattered across the blue flesh, like grains of coarse pepper. But as quickly as they appeared they closed up again.

A line of bullet holes sliced downwards across the end of a tentacle. The tip was cut from the main limb, flopping to the floor. But it was a hollow victory – the end of the tentacle throbbed and jumped, almost hitting a soldier, who stumbled back from it, face drained of colour.

'Back door!' Jack was yelling. 'Everyone out the back.'

'So long as there aren't more of them waiting there,' Rose shouted.

Jack grabbed her arm. 'You're no fun,' he complained as they ran for the counter.

They dived over, to find the Doctor sitting on the floor the other side. He was holding a bottle of the colourless spirit that everyone seemed addicted to. He bit the cork and wrenched it out with his teeth.

'It's not that bad yet,' she told him.

'We need to slow them down a bit,' the Doctor said.

There was a splintering explosion from the other side of the inn. Rose risked a look, ducking away as a tentacle smacked past. But she had seen enough – the creature was inside now, and others were clustered outside the windows, pressing heavily against what was left of the glass.

'You're telling me,' Rose said.

Jack was on his feet again, encouraging everyone out through the back of the inn and shouting at the remaining soldiers to leave.

'Those other bottles,' the Doctor said to Rose, nodding up at the shelves behind the bar.

'You want 'em?'

'Nah – give them to Mr Blob out there.'

She didn't need telling twice. Rose grabbed bottle after bottle off the shelf and hurled them at the approaching creature. Most bounced off the gelatinous flesh, but smashed as they hit the floor. A mass of writhing tentacles slapped past Rose, fumbling towards her.

'Time we were going,' she warned the Doctor.

Jack was standing in the doorway beside the bar, shouting at them to hurry.

The Doctor pulled himself to his feet and made his way over in a leisurely fashion to join Jack and Rose. 'Anyone got a lighter?' he asked.

Jack slapped a silver cigarette lighter into his palm.

'Might have known it would be you.' The Doctor examined it appreciatively, angling it so he could read the inscription engraved on the side. 'To Squiffy from Smudger. Thanks for everything.' He raised an eyebrow.

Jack shrugged. 'Just something I picked up. Present.' He stepped smartly aside to allow a blue tentacle to flop past. 'Soon would be good, you know.'

The Doctor flicked the lighter. 'Right part of the world for a Molotov Cocktail, I s'pose.' He held up the bottle and watched the flames as they sputtered and grew, traces of black smoke curling up from them.

Then he hurled the bottle at the creature that was now hauling itself over the counter to get at them.

'Run!'

The room exploded into flames. The creature was shrieking, wailing, thrashing. Rose thought she could see it melting – glutinous blue liquid rolling viscous down its sides. But she didn't wait to be sure.

* * *

The land behind the inn was raised up above most of the village and the harbour, midway between floodplain and cliffs. The soldiers stood in a circle protecting the few villagers, and the Doctor, Rose and Jack were with Levin at the edge of the circle.

Below them, through the thin veil of mist, Rose could see the creatures moving slowly through the village – there seemed to be dozens of them. Large, glowing bodies slithered along, tentacles reaching in front of them as they felt their way forwards.

'Door to door,' Levin snapped to his men. 'Get the villagers out.'

'Take them to the base,' the Doctor said.

'Won't the things go there?' Rose said. 'I mean, there's power and light – everything they're hunting for.'

'People too,' the Doctor agreed. 'But we won't survive out in this cold for long.'

'So what's the plan?' Jack asked.

'Get everyone to the base. See if we can get Georgi to keep the monsters at bay.'

Jack nodded. 'I'll help Levin.'

Colonel Levin sent one of his men off at a run to get to the base and bring more of the soldiers back to help with the evacuation. The rest of them – including Jack and Levin himself – headed for the village. The Doctor and Rose took charge of the civilians from the pub, and started the long, cold journey up the cliff path and across to the research institute.

Rose took Georgi's hand to lead him. He pulled away at first, then seemed to accept the help. 'I know you,' he said in his cracked, brittle voice. 'The girl who came to see me when Nikolai died.'

'Yeah, Rose.'

'A pretty name.' Georgi nodded, his white stick tapping ahead on the narrow pathway. 'Don't let him kill me,' he said quietly.

'Him?' Rose shook her head, even though he couldn't see. 'No, it's the things from... from underground. But we'll keep you safe. All of you.'

The old man gripped her hand more tightly. 'Not them. I can feel them, I know they are there. It's *him* I fear. The bad wolf. The man I see in my dreams – waking and sleeping. The man who will kill me.' He turned as if to look at Rose, his eyes almost completely white in the night. The flames from the harbour below flickered on his pale face. 'The man with the wolf on his arm.'

They split up, running from house to house, trying to keep ahead of the creatures. Fortunately the village sprawled out from the harbour and the soldiers were able to get to most houses before the creatures did. Most, but not all.

Jack saw one house all but flattened by several of the creatures. They oozed and squelched through the rubble, pulsing with renewed energy. He didn't let himself stop to wonder where they had come from, how many people had died. He ran to the next house, hammering on the door, shouting into the night.

And then on to the next house.

And the next.

A long line of tired, frightened people hurried through the snow, heading for the cliffs and out of immediate danger. But for how long, Jack wondered?

'That's it!' someone shouted. 'These are the last.'

Several soldiers were leading a ragged group of people from the far end of the village. Dark shapes against the white snow.

'You sure that's the lot?' Jack asked them.

'Yes, sir. If there's anyone else, it's too late. Those things are coming at us from both sides now. We need to get moving.'

Jack nodded. 'Come on, then.'

They hurried the few villagers along, encouraging and helping them. Further up the road, Jack could see Levin with another group of villagers and soldiers. Beyond that was the dark shape of the base. He turned and looked back – saw the fires still burning down in the harbour; the creatures moving through the village behind them, going from house to house as he himself had done...

'Right, let's get a move on,' Jack shouted. 'It's not far now, then we'll be safe.'

'How can you be sure?' someone wondered.

'I've got a friend,' Jack replied. 'He'll help me sort this out.'

'Can anyone?' another voice queried. 'Can anyone sort out what is happening to us here?'

Jack turned to the man, intending to reassure him. The distant firelight threw a pale-orange glow onto the man's wrinkled face. It was a face he knew. A father who had already all but lost his daughter. Jack forced a smile and clapped the man on the shoulder.

'Mamentov,' he said, 'you have been through a lot, I know. But believe me…' He stopped, frowning. Jack had been glancing round at the other people as he spoke. But – he couldn't see her. 'Where's Valeria?' Jack asked quietly, feeling suddenly numb. 'Where's your daughter?'

Mamentov held Jack's gaze for a moment, then looked away. 'I have no daughter.'

Jack swallowed. 'They got her? We were too late?'

The old man turned back, his face set and determined as he spoke. 'I have no daughter,' he repeated. 'Not any more. What use is she now? She does nothing – just sits and stares. I even have to feed her, and…' He shook his head. 'I have no daughter,' he said again, quiet and sad and final.

Jack just stared at him. Overlaid on the old man's defiant face he could see the face of the girl – just as old and lined, but empty and devoid of emotion. Drained – everything taken from her. 'You left her behind, didn't you?' Jack said. 'You left her behind for those things to get.' His mouth was dry and there was a tightness in his stomach. 'You heartless, selfish moron!'

'You can't go back there, sir,' one of the soldiers shouted. 'You can't go back!'

But Jack wasn't listening. He was running down the hill, towards the village and the sounds of destruction as the creatures moved through it. Hunting.

He wasn't thinking, just running. Hoping he could

remember where Mamentov's house was, skirting the village, keeping well away from the glowing creatures as they slithered and scrambled through the deserted streets. The mist was drifting in as the last of the street lights flickered and went out.

A shadow detached itself from the darkness and flew at Jack. It caught him squarely in the chest, heaving him backwards – out of the way of the tentacle that slashed through the air where he had been a moment earlier. The tentacle slapped to the ground, pulled back, disappeared into the night. Jack could see the pale glow of the creature moving off into the distance.

'Thank you,' Jack gasped, winded, looking up at his saviour.

'You deserved it,' came the reply. Sergeyev was looking down at him. He offered Jack his hand and pulled him to his feet. 'Now we're all square.'

'You got out of the sub, then,' Jack said. 'Obviously.'

'Yes. Thank you.'

'You'd better get after the others.' Jack pointed into the darkness. 'Colonel Levin's evacuated the villagers, or as many as we could. They're making for the base.'

'But what about you?'

'I'll be there. There's something I have to do first.'

'Maybe I can help.'

Jack met the man's gaze. He remembered how scathing Sergeyev had been of Jack's sympathy for Valeria – how that was what had sparked their initial row. 'I don't think so.'

'Tell me,' Sergeyev insisted.

'The old man, Mamentov – he's left his daughter behind.'

'That mindless girl?'

Jack nodded.

'He saved himself and left her.' Sergeyev turned to look into the darkness, towards the base and safety. 'I understand.'

'I thought you would,' Jack snapped. 'You're as callous as he is.'

But Sergeyev laughed.

Jack gritted his teeth. 'It's not funny.'

'No,' Sergeyev said, suddenly serious. 'You think I understand the old man. That isn't what I meant.'

'What did you mean, then?'

'I meant that I understand you, my friend. Come on.' He set off into the darkness, towards the village. 'Let's find her before it's too late.'

The villagers were hustled into the base, told briefly what was happening and asked to help if they could. Those who were not too old or frightened or inebriated joined Levin's troops on the road. The Doctor left Levin to organise things, knowing that Jack would help when he returned from the village.

They were building a bonfire. A huge pile of anything they could find that would burn. Drums of fuel oil were rolled round from the back of the institute where the generators were. Inside, the villagers and scientists ripped out anything flammable and piled it outside to be moved down to the fire.

'We need to keep back enough to run the generators until we can get help,' Levin told Lieutenant Krylek. 'I don't want to live through this only to die of the cold in a few days' time.'

'You think the Doctor's plan will work, sir?' Krylek asked quietly.

Levin's reply was just as quiet. 'I really don't know. But it gives us something to do. And, crazy though it seems, I don't have any better ideas.'

The road was on a narrow, raised area of land at the point where they were building the fire. The sides were almost sheer – dropping away nearly twenty metres either side. The pile of debris stretched almost across the narrow plateau now. Fedor Vahlen had driven his digger up from the village. Its headlight cut through the misty night as he dumped load after load of broken furniture, ripped-up carpet, desk tops, anything that would burn, onto the pile.

With the last of the villagers and soldiers arriving, Levin called everyone to the institute side of the pyre. 'I want this roadway blocked off completely,' he said. 'No way through. If the Doctor is right and Georgi can lead these things mindlessly along and into the flames, then I don't want any of them coming round the side.'

The creatures seemed to be everywhere. Jack could hear them slithering in the darkness, could see the blue glow from them illuminating the sky ahead like the lights from a distant city.

'That's the house,' Sergeyev said.

They were almost there now. A quick dash across an area of open ground. Jack and Sergeyev crouched in the doorway.

'Looks like we're in time,' Sergeyev said. 'Go and get her. I'll keep watch.'

Jack flung the door open and leaped into the small front room of the house. It was empty. He didn't want to try the lights – they probably wouldn't work, and if they did would only draw the attention of the creatures. Back room – nothing. A small kitchen with the tap dripping. No sign of Valeria.

'Quickly!' Sergeyev called through the open door. 'I can hear one of them coming.'

'How close?' Jack yelled back.

Stairs – two at a time. Narrow and steep.

'I don't know. Can't see it.'

Top landing – barely room to stand. Three doors. First room.

Empty.

Second room.

Empty.

'My God – it's on the roof!'

A crash of breaking glass.

Third room – the tentacle smashing through the window and lashing back and forth. Jack stood in the doorway watching, unable to get to the bed. Unable to reach the girl lying there, unmoving, staring silently at the ceiling. She was oblivious to the creature, the danger, the world around her.

'Leave her,' Jack thought. 'I'll have to leave her.' And

he dived across the room, under the tentacle, sliding along the bare boards towards the bed.

Gunfire from outside. The tentacle hesitated. Then withdrew.

'Sergeyev – I've got her. Get out of it, get away.'

More gunfire.

Then silence.

Jack had Valeria across his shoulders, surprised how heavy she was. He stumbled out of the room, almost falling down the steep stairs. Out into the darkness.

Darkness tinged with blue. Creatures all around, as if watching the house.

And in the middle of them, outside the door, Sergeyev staring sightlessly at the night sky. His gun by his side and his face crumpled and pale like an old paper bag.

Jack gritted his teeth. Reached up with his free hand to pat Valeria's unfeeling head. 'We'll be OK. I promise.'

Then Jack was running for their lives.

Klebanov had suggested the Clean Room. The Doctor wanted somewhere isolated and quiet where Georgi could concentrate, away from distractions. The Clean Room was a glass cage in the corner of a large, bare room. Just a wooden desk and an office chair remained. There was a complicated electronic locking system on the double set of doors that acted as an airlock, operated from a numeric keypad. The glass was bullet- and blast-proof. The cage was empty apart from several gas canisters piled up at the back of the room. They were stamped with a red skull and crossbones.

'It is where we used to work on contagious bacteria,' Klebanov told the Doctor, Rose and Georgi.

'We still have some, as you can see.' Minin pointed to the canisters. 'This seemed the best place to keep the stuff. With the doors closed it's completely sealed.'

'Can't you destroy it?' Rose asked. 'Or, I dunno, send it back?'

'No one wants it back,' Klebanov told her.

'Decommission it? Make it safe?' the Doctor suggested.

'The equipment for that went long ago,' Alex Minin explained. 'Traded for other supplies. More urgent things like food and oil.'

Klebanov grunted, but did not disagree. 'Will it do?'

The Doctor grinned. 'It's great. Let's find Georgi here a chair. Then I'll have a little talk to him. After that we have a few other things to do while he gets on with it.'

'Like what?' Rose wanted to know.

'Like checking on our bonfire. Like burning a few blobs.'

Minin opened the door by tapping a code into the keypad. He carried the chair from the desk through into the area between the two doors, closing the outer door behind him. Then he tapped the code into the keypad within the airlock and the inner door clicked open. He put down the chair.

'Let's get started.' The Doctor led Georgi to the door. 'What's the code?'

'1917,' Klebanov told him.

'What else?' The Doctor tapped it in and led Georgi through.

Once he was seated in the chair, the Doctor spoke quietly to him. He put his fingers to the old man's temples, relaxing him, putting him into a trance. Minin watched with interest.

After a while, the Doctor stepped away. He put his finger to his lips as Minin made to speak and nodded at the door. The two of them left the cage, Georgi sitting inside, alone, staring at the glass wall in front of him.

'Someone should stay with him,' the Doctor said.

'I'll do it,' Rose replied at once.

'No, I need you with me. Minin – can I trust you?'

'I hope so, Doctor.'

'I hope so too.'

'What do I need to do?'

'Probably nothing. Just make sure he's all right. There a phone in here?'

Klebanov went to the bare desk on the other side of the room. In a drawer he found a phone and plugged it into a wall socket. He lifted the receiver to check it was connected. 'Extension 514.'

'I'll need the full number,' the Doctor said. 'Any problems, I'll call you on Rose's mobile. You can give Georgi new instructions to pass on to the blob things. He's in a receptive state. You won't know it, but he'll hear you.'

'Will it get a signal? None of the radios are working,' Klebanov pointed out.

'Super phone,' Rose told him. 'It'll work.'

Klebanov gave the Doctor the number. Minin sat on the desk, watching Georgi. 'Will he just sit there, like that?'

'I hope so. Come on, Rose – work to do.'

Klebanov followed the Doctor and Rose to the door. Then he paused and turned back to Minin. 'It could be a long night,' he said. 'Get yourself a coffee. I'll wait here with Georgi till you get back.'

'So what's going to happen?' Rose asked.

They crossed the paved compound outside the institute and started down the road.

'Georgi has managed to get on the same wavelength as the ship's psychic communication with the remotes.'

'Like when he saw what they were up to before?'

'Right. Only this time he's talking to them. I hope he's filtering out the ship's messages and adding his own instructions.'

'So, he's, like, hacked in?'

'Yeah. He's hacked in. And he's telling them all to come here.'

'To get us?'

'Well, not really. That's what they think – so far as they think at all. But they just do what he tells them now. And he's telling them to come along this road and keep going. Into that.'

The Doctor pointed to the massive pile ahead of them blocking the road and stretching across the narrow ridge.

'And that'll stop them?'

'Will when it's on fire. They like the cold. Any energy they draw doesn't come through as heat because it's passed straight on. The shock of a sudden temperature change as they go into the fire ought to deactivate 'em all. Can't really kill 'em cos they're not really alive, you see.'

'Ought to,' Rose echoed.

'Yeah.'

'Bonfire night and a half, then.'

'Yeah.'

'So when do we light the blue touch-paper?'

'Soon as we see them coming.'

They had reached Levin and his men, standing looking at their work. The colonel turned to the Doctor, hearing his last comment. 'They're coming now,' he said. 'Look.' He pointed past the side of the pyre, into the valley below. A line of glowing blue was vaguely visible through the drifting mist.

'Charges are set,' Lieutenant Krylek reported. 'We can light her up as soon as you're ready.'

The Doctor was looking down into the valley, watching the blue glow edge slowly closer, wondering where Jack had got to.

'Let's do it,' he said.

Uphill was bad news. Jack had to put the girl down. She could stand. She could walk. She just didn't seem to know she was doing it. Just stared straight ahead into the misty darkness and let Jack lead her.

Running seemed like too much to ask. She was a

sleepwalker – no sign of consciousness, just one foot in front of the other. Her old face framed by young hair was devoid of expression. Her eyes showed no flicker of recognition as Jack urged her onwards. He held her by the hand, pulling her along as fast as he could.

If he went too fast, she stumbled and fell. She made no effort to save herself, and her clothes were soaked from the snow, her face scratched, her hair dishevelled. Least of her problems, Jack decided.

He was out of breath, nearly exhausted. 'Not far now,' he gasped, though he knew he was only saying it for his own benefit. 'Just up the hill. Almost there.'

But behind them he could see a line of the creatures starting up the road in pursuit. Were they really following? Did they know Jack and the girl were there – could they sense them? Or were they just making for the institute at the other end of the road?

Jack and Valeria were struggling along a narrowing ridge. At the sides of the road, the land dropped away into deeper darkness. Jack could only tell because the pale glint of the snow just stopped where the ridge ended. 'Come on,' he encouraged Valeria – could she hear him? Probably not. But he said it anyway: 'Come on. Not far. Almost there. We'll be all right in a few minutes.'

Behind them the creatures were edging closer, catching up.

Ahead of them the night exploded.

Fire leaping high and wide as the entire ridge burst into flames. The heat of it almost knocked Jack backwards. The whole ridge was burning, the snow retreating from the heat as it melted and evaporated from the roadway. There was no way they could get through to the institute now.

But perhaps the heat would drive the creatures back. 'They don't like fire and heat,' Jack reassured Valeria. Her expression did not change. He squeezed her unfeeling hand. 'We'll be fine now. They'll turn back. You'll see. Any moment now.'

But the creatures kept coming.

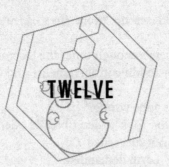

TWELVE

The Doctor was counting on his fingers, peering through the smoke and flames. It made Rose's eyes sting and she blinked and squinted.

'Thought there'd be more of them,' the Doctor was saying.

She couldn't look. The smoke was everywhere, thick and black from the fuel oil. Rose had to turn away. And as she did so, as she blinked and coughed and the tears ran down her cheeks, she could see the institute framed against the night sky behind them. The firelight was a flickering orange across its blank concrete façade. But it was an orange tinged with blue.

From either side, across the snow-clad fields and from the cliff top, far in the distance the creatures were coming. She pulled at the Doctor's sleeve. 'Look.'

'It's great, isn't it?' He was still staring into the flames. 'We've got 'em licked.'

'We haven't got 'em licked. Look.' She pulled harder.

'They've come round the sides,' he said quietly.

'We could set up more fires,' Lieutenant Krylek suggested.

'Doubt there's enough time,' the Doctor told him.

Levin was nodding in agreement. 'And we've nothing left to burn.'

'So what's gone wrong?'

The Doctor took a deep breath. 'Georgi,' he said. 'Either he's not succeeded. Or…'

'Or what?' Levin demanded.

'Barinska wasn't working alone.' He clicked his fingers. 'Phone.'

Rose handed him her mobile and he punched the buttons. He was already running, back towards the institute. 'Keep the fire burning,' he shouted at Levin. 'Maybe we can still lead them here.'

They were huddled as close to the flames as Jack could stand. Valeria didn't object, didn't seem to feel the heat or appreciate the danger. And still the creatures edged closer. Jack reckoned they had maybe ten minutes. At most. Then he would have to drag Valeria to her feet, maybe carry her, run for it – hope to get through the mass of glowing blue flesh that was rolling up the roadway towards them.

'Fat chance,' he murmured.

He held her tight, arm round her shoulder. There was no give at all, no recognition or reaction. It was like holding a corpse.

The sound of the phone in the quiet of the room

startled Minin. It took him a moment to recover, then he snatched at the receiver in sudden excitement.

'Doctor? Has it worked? Have we done it?'

But he could tell at once from the Doctor's tone that things were not going well. 'What's Georgi doing? Can't he concentrate? Has he woken from the trance?'

Minin looked into the glass cage. 'No. He's just sitting there. Looks like he might be muttering something. But he's not moved. Not at all.'

'Then he's still in contact. Alex – you have to break the contact. He's bringing the creatures round the side. He's bypassed the fire. He's leading them right to us.'

Minin felt cold. 'Stop him? How?'

'Any way you can. We'll be right with you. But – every second counts.'

The phone went dead. Minin put down the handset slowly, considering.

He could see them, rolling up the hill and coming along the road. He could feel the heat of the fire, and he wondered how soon the other fires would be lit.

'Don't bring them all up the road,' the voice had said. Whispering to him as he concentrated, as he felt the tingle of the creatures in his mind's eye. 'Make sure most of them come round the sides, otherwise they will expect a trap. We'll lay other fires for them, don't worry. Just concentrate on bringing them to us. Bringing them here.' It was a soft, kind voice. Assured and confident. 'Don't worry about anything else. Just bring them here. To us.'

The outside world did not exist. Just the creatures – slithering ever closer. If Georgi could hear Minin's shouts from the other side of the thick glass, if he could hear the hammering on the wall, it meant nothing to him.

'The creatures – bring them here.'

That was his whole world…

No reaction. The man obviously couldn't – or wouldn't – hear him. Minin hammered with his fists on the glass. Then he reached inside his jacket and took out a pistol. He had taken it from his desk drawer when Klebanov sent him to get coffee. In the old days, Minin carried it all the time. He feared for his life all the time. He hadn't even looked at it for years, hadn't fired it since… He was confident the Doctor knew what he was doing, but even so Minin had decided he wanted the gun. He knew it would have no effect on the creatures, but then it was not them he was intending to use it on if things turned really bad. It was his insurance. His way out. His only way out.

1917. The outer door clicked open. Minin stepped into the airlock. After a moment, the outer door closed behind him. He reached out for the keypad on the internal door. His hands were sweating. The gun felt slippery. He'd only ever killed a man once before. Surely it wouldn't come to that. Surely the threat would be enough. An old blind man – shake him by the shoulder, push him off the chair if need be. Just break the link.

1917. Nothing. Just a bleep of protest.

The door remained closed. He must have keyed the number in wrong. His eyes were swimming, vision blurred. His finger was slippery with perspiration – might have slid on to the wrong button. He tried again.

And again.

The code didn't work. It had worked only minutes before. Could someone have changed the setting, overridden the code? He hammered on the door with the butt of the pistol. Still no reaction from the old man. With a sigh of frustration, Minin turned round and punched the code into the outer door. He'd have to wait for the Doctor. The Doctor would know what to do.

1917.

Bleep.

The outer door remained closed. Trapping Minin between two sheets of bullet-proof glass. Inside the cage, Georgi continued to mutter, to guide the creatures towards the institute. Oblivious.

The Doctor took in the situation at a glance. Georgi sat motionless inside the glass cage. Minin hammering on the outer door – trapped in the airlock.

'Get Vahlen,' he told Rose.

'Who?'

'Guy in the digger. He's an engineer. Tell him to bring his tools.'

'But can't you –'

'You want a debate, or you want to help?' he snapped,

handing her back her mobile. 'Get him. I'll do what I can.'

She nodded and ran.

The Doctor pulled out his sonic screwdriver and went straight to the keypad by the door. Old technology – antiquated. Could he persuade it to work for him?

'1917.' Minin's voice was faint but audible. 'It works from that side.'

The Doctor nodded and keyed in the code. A bleep from the system. 'Not any more.' He set to work with the screwdriver and a shower of sparks erupted from the keypad. 'That doesn't look good,' he admitted, waving away the curls of smoke. The keypad was a twisted, melted mess. 'Whoops,' he said quietly.

'Should we pull back inside the base?' Krylek asked.

'Safer here by the fire,' Levin told him. 'I think.'

'Then should we evacuate the civilians and scientists, bring them here?'

Levin looked across to where the line of blue was moving ever closer to the institute. 'I doubt there's time. Let's pray the Doctor stops them.'

He sounded more hopeful than he felt. Rose was running across from the base towards them. She was shouting something – good news? Please let it be good news.

'Where's the guy on the digger?' she gasped as she got closer.

'What?'

'Quick – we need him.'

Levin simply pointed. Close to the raging fire, the shape of the digger was just visible through the billowing smoke.

'Thanks.' And with no further explanation, Rose set off towards it.

'Why don't they stop?' Jack asked out loud. 'Why doesn't the heat drive them off?'

The nearest of the creatures was melting like jelly – rivulets of molten blue running down the glutinous sides. A tentacle whipped out, towards the flames – crashed past Jack's head. When it withdrew, it was burning. The creature shrieked in pain, the end of the tentacle a mass of flames. But still it kept coming.

'Sorry about this,' Jack said quietly, close to the girl's ear.

She did not reply.

The burning tentacle lashed out again – right at them.

The keypad for the internal door detached from the mechanism behind it. Minin had pulled it away and was ripping out wires in response to the Doctor's shouted instructions. He cried out in alarm and surprise as a jolt of power ran through his fingers.

'That'll be live, so careful,' the Doctor called to him.

'Thanks.' Minin sucked his fingertips. 'Now I reconnect it to which one?'

The Doctor told him. 'Dunno if it'll work, mind.'

He twisted the wire together. 'Now what?'

'Key in 1789 and see what happens.'

'Why 1789?' he asked as he pressed the buttons, hoping it would work.

'Seemed like an appropriate number.'

No bleep. Instead the hiss of the door mechanism. It clicked open. Minin sighed with relief. The Doctor was grinning at him through the glass door.

The inner door opened an inch. Two inches. Three. Painfully slowly. Four inches.

Then it stopped.

Minin pushed. No movement. Jammed. He shoved at it. Put his shoulder to the door and heaved.

Without effect.

She paused for a moment to catch her breath. Vahlen had caught the urgency of Rose's instructions from the Doctor and climbed down from the digger. He took a tool box from the back of the vehicle and set off towards the base.

Rose wanted to tell him to get a move on, but she was so out of breath she could scarcely speak. The smoke clawed at the back of her throat as she drew in great rasping gulps of air. It made her cough.

Leaning against the digger, she stared into the flames of the huge bonfire. Through the flickering firelight she could see the blue glow of the creatures as they moved slowly but inexorably towards the fire. The Doctor had been right – if only they could direct the rest of the things into the fire they might still have a chance.

Having caught her breath, Rose turned to follow

Vahlen. Then paused. Movement – out of the corner of her eye as she turned she had seen movement. From the other side of the fire. Not the blue glow of the advancing creatures, but a dark silhouette moving quickly to escape a thrashing, burning tentacle. Rose leaned as close as she could to the fire.

Was there someone there – trapped on the other side? If there was, she could do nothing for them. She peered through the smoke and flames, struggling to make sense of the shapes and movement on the other side…

The phone was ringing again. It had to be Rose. The Doctor snatched it up. 'Yeah?'

Minin was struggling with the door. He could just get his hand through the gap, but he couldn't open it any further.

Rose was shouting in the Doctor's ear. Telling him the creatures were almost there. That Jack was on the other side of the fire and they had to help him. That time was running out. What she was going to do.

The Doctor did not reply. He hung up the phone. 'See you,' he said quietly. 'Good luck.' Then he was back at the door, shouting to Minin. 'You've got to stop him. Those creatures are nearly here. Get the door open and stop him!'

But the door wasn't moving. Minin stared back at the Doctor, face gaunt – haunted, hollow-eyed – as he slipped off his jacket and pushed up his sleeves. He held the gun in his left hand – so he could squeeze it through the gap between the door and the frame, could reach round to aim at Georgi sitting silent and still in the cage.

On Minin's forearm was tattooed a snarling wolf. Despite being muffled by the thick glass, the sound of the shot echoed round the room.

This was it. Jack had wrapped himself round the girl, protecting her as best he could, though he wasn't sure why he was bothering. At least she would feel nothing as the creatures grabbed her and drew out what was left of her life.

A tentacle clawed at Jack's arm, wrapping round, heaving him away from the girl. He hung on, pulling her with him. 'We'll go together,' he said, teeth gritted. He felt woozy, tired, as if he'd not slept for a month...

A triumphant roar – like a massive engine straining in too low a gear. He looked up, expecting to see the creature bearing down on him.

Instead it was knocked away, the tentacle ripped from Jack's arm, and suddenly he was awake and alert – and watching the massive digger that smashed into the creature and set it tumbling backwards. The huge wheels were on fire, rubber tyres showering sparks as they turned.

It reversed, back towards Jack and Valeria. The figure in the cab was waving and shouting. Rose.

He couldn't hear her, but he didn't need to. There was only one thing to do. The creatures were advancing again – gathering themselves as if to leap forwards.

Jack heaved the girl into his arms and stumbled to the digger. He collapsed with her into the metal scoop at the front. There was a hiss and he could smell his clothes singe. Wisps of grey smoke were curling upwards and the heat was soaking through from the hot metal and into him. He almost cried out with the pain, gritting his teeth. Valeria was a dead weight on top of him. He had to keep her from getting burned – she wouldn't feel it, wouldn't know to pull away from the hot surfaces.

The engine roared again and Jack was being lifted. The scoop was rising slowly up into the air. Flames danced round them, but thin and pale. From the top of the fire as Rose drove back through.

Then there was a loud explosion and the world lurched to one side. A tyre, he realised – blown out by the heat. The digger lurched forwards. Stopped. Lurched again. Slowly the scoop was lowering and Rose's smoke-stained face was waiting, looking down at him as Jack rolled out onto the mercifully cold ground. Valeria lay beside him, staring impassively up at the smoky sky.

'Hot date?' Rose said.

'Too hot,' he told her. 'Even for me.' He pulled himself to his feet and dusted down his ruined coat. 'Hey,' he said. 'Thanks.'

Minin could not easily reach round far enough to fire at Georgi. He hoped the shot would wake the man, break his concentration.

It didn't.

He struggled to force more of his arm through, to be able to angle it so he could shoot the man. Shoot him. Had it come to that – shooting an old man? Would just wounding him be enough? Could he do it?

From the other side of the glass, the Doctor was shouting. But Minin could not make out the words. All he could hear was the blood rushing in his ears. All he could see was Chedakin's laughing face. He blinked it away, aimed as best he could.

Fired.

The shot missed again. Georgi did not move. There was another noise now, not just the rushing of blood – a hissing. Like escaping gas.

Gas.

And Minin could see the dark puncture mark in the canister behind Georgi. A thick red mist was seeping out. A cloud of scarlet gathering in the air, rolling lazily across the room.

Last chance. He shot again, unthinking, unfeeling. The cloud was engulfing Georgi now. The old man slumped forwards. Minin heard the crash of his body hitting the floor. He ripped his arm back through the gap. Punched at the keypad. 'Close, damn you – close!'

The door didn't move.

The red mist was spreading slowly across the room towards him...

'He's killed Georgi,' Vahlen said. His voice was flat –

shocked out of any inflection.

'He didn't mean to,' the Doctor said gently. 'He was trying to warn him, or just wound him. Now get Minin out of there before he dies too.'

'What is it?' Vahlen pointed to the red mist.

'Deadly. Can you get the door open? Get him out?'

Vahlen examined the fused keypad. Minin's face was close to his, through the glass. Eyes wide with fear.

'Probably.' But Vahlen made no effort to do it. 'He betrayed Chedakin,' he said quietly. 'Betrayed my friend. He deserves to die.'

'No one deserves to die.'

'What about Georgi?'

'He didn't deserve it either. But there was no other way.'

'And Chedakin?'

The Doctor hauled Vahlen to his feet. His dark eyes stared into the man's very soul. 'You still don't get it, do you? You saw the file in his office. You still think that Minin drove your innocent friend to suicide?'

'What else?'

The red mist was halfway across the room. Minin was hammering on the door.

'There was a party agent working undercover, sending back information. Damning you all.'

'Minin.'

'No!'

'Then he worked for Minin.'

'You saw the memos. Minin didn't even know he was here. And when he found out...'

And Vahlen did see it then. 'Chedakin? But he was my friend.'

'He would have betrayed you all,' the Doctor said. 'That's why Minin shot him. Back of the head. An unlikely suicide. More of an execution.'

'I thought he was my friend,' Vahlen said weakly.

'Then hurry up and save the man who never told you different.' The Doctor lifted up the tool box, holding it open for Vahlen. 'Do it.'

The troops were retreating into the base. Pretty soon the creatures would be there, and Levin knew his men would be trapped between creatures and fire. Their only chance was to get inside and try to defend the concrete building.

Rose and Jack were with them. Jack was carrying Valeria in his arms, stumbling across the compound.

Once inside, Rose led Jack and Valeria to the Doctor. Levin and his men immediately started to barricade the doors and block off the windows. Krylek had gone to get the civilians to help.

The Doctor was in the corridor, with a sullen-looking Vahlen. Alex Minin stumbled after them. He looked pale and frightened and was clutching a handkerchief to his mouth as if he was afraid he was going to be sick.

'They're almost here,' Rose said.

'Levin's barricading us in, so I hope you've got a plan,' Jack added. Beside him, Valeria stood staring blankly forwards.

'Is she all right?' Minin asked hesitantly.

'No,' Jack told him.

'But the rest of us will be,' the Doctor said. He was smiling. 'It's risky, but we'll have to try to shut the ship down. At least we know now there's a direct link.'

'What about Georgi?' Minin asked.

'You did the right thing. The only thing. I dunno why he was bringing the creatures here. Maybe he was in with Barinska, cos someone was. But whatever, it's time to finish this.'

He led the way down the corridor, and Rose realised they were heading back to the storeroom where the tunnel to the ship emerged. 'But didn't you say it was dangerous to try to shut down the ship?'

'Oh, yes. Very.' He was suddenly serious. 'While there was another way, I'd never have risked it. But now it's our only chance. This is Plan B.'

'And there's no Plan C,' Jack said.

'That's right.'

The door to the storeroom was still standing open. On the other side of the room, the hidden door was closed, and the Doctor went over to it. 'You don't have to come with me,' he told them all.

'You might need help,' Jack said.

'We're coming,' Rose told him.

'Great.' He pulled open the door.

And a huge tentacle hurtled towards him.

The Doctor slammed the door shut again, but it caught on the tentacle, which was forcing its way into the room. The door burst open – a glowing, blue, glutinous mass filling the frame behind. Forcing its way through into the storeroom.

'Back!' Jack shouted, shoving Valeria ahead of him.

The Doctor was last out, slamming the door behind them.

'That won't stop it,' Minin said. He seemed to be shivering.

'Not for long, no.'

'So what now?' Rose said.

The Doctor looked at her, meeting her gaze. 'Back to the main doors,' he said. 'It's time for Plan C.'

THIRTEEN

'If we're lucky we can keep them out for a while,' Levin was saying.

He and Krylek and several of the soldiers were standing by the barricaded main doors. Metal filing cabinets were jammed up against them – most of the barricade was metal, made from things that had been left behind because they wouldn't burn on the fire.

'Too late – they're already inside,' the Doctor said, running up. 'Sorry.'

'So what now?'

'Working on Plan C,' Rose told him.

'Minin's looking for plans of the building, so let's get to his office. Everyone else to the conference room. At least we'll all be together,' the Doctor said. 'Jack's already assembling all the civilians he can find. Get your men to help him.'

'You think there's another way out, sir?' Krylek asked.

'Nope,' the Doctor told him. 'I think there may be somewhere to hide.'

The barricade shuddered under a blow from outside. An upended metal desk toppled away and crashed to the floor. Dust showered down from the ceiling.

'There's one on the roof,' Levin said.

In Alex Minin's office, Boris Brodsky and Catherine Kornilova watched Klebanov arguing with Minin.

'Those plans are out of date, they're no help at all,' the chief scientist was saying.

'They're all we have.'

'They're from the 1960s, for goodness' sake!'

'Children,' Jack admonished. He had sat Valeria in an upright plastic chair on the other side of the room. He'd left the civilians in the conference room, together with most of the soldiers, but he didn't trust Valeria's father to look after her.

The Doctor arrived with Levin and the soldiers. 'Post guards along the corridors. Let us know as soon as the creatures are in.'

'That one in the storeroom seems to be staying put for now,' Jack told them.

'Waiting for its mates,' Rose said.

'Could be,' the Doctor agreed. 'Right – what have we here?'

Jack and the other scientists moved aside to let him get to the desk where Minin and Klebanov were arguing about the plans.

'What are you looking for?' Minin asked.

Levin joined them. 'I don't see a way out,' he said, scanning the maps.

The Doctor traced his finger round the main corridor. 'See this? It runs right round the edge of the building. Rooms off either side. This is us, here. That's your office, Klebanov. That's the conference room. Labs. Storerooms.'

'So?' Klebanov demanded. 'It shows us nothing we don't know.'

'Maybe not.' The Doctor jabbed his finger down in the middle of the floor plan. 'Right here. In the middle. What's this?'

'It's… nothing,' Minin said. 'There's nothing marked.'

'Must be something,' the Doctor told him.

The other two scientists – Boris Brodsky and Catherine Kornilova – were leaning in to look.

'I've never been there,' Brodsky said. 'There's no way in.'

'Nothing to do with the labs,' Catherine added. 'Probably just a closed-off area or solid concrete. The building's in the shape of a square with a courtyard or something, except there's no way into it.'

Levin was running his finger along the same route the Doctor had traced. 'Everything's round the edge. But I've seen this place from above, when we arrived in the helicopter. It's solid. Completely enclosed. The Doctor's right – there is something there.' He pointed to a storeroom. 'This is the access point. A corridor blocked off and turned into a room. Another one here.'

'So what are you saying?' Rose wanted to know. 'Is it just empty space or what?'

'Might be full of concrete,' Jack pointed out. 'Solid.'

'Nope.' The Doctor pulled out a plan from underneath the one they were looking at. 'Wiring, pipes, air conditioning – they all service that area like any other.'

'You're wondering why it is blocked off,' Klebanov said quietly.

'Yes. But I'm also thinking it's the best place to defend, *because* it's blocked off.'

Klebanov was shaking his head. 'Go in there,' he said, 'and you're dead.'

The barricade finally collapsed. One of the filing cabinets split open, spilling papers across the floor. The doors were bulging, bursting. A blue wall pulsed and glowed beyond them.

The two soldiers left on guard retreated slowly along the corridor, their rifles levelled even though they knew they were useless against the creature that was now forcing its way inside.

They turned to run. But not quite quickly enough. A tentacle shot across the corridor, swiping one of the soldiers off his feet. His comrade paused, turned, watched as his friend was dragged away – face collapsing and limbs atrophying. He hesitated only for a moment, then he ran.

The Doctor was facing Klebanov. The room was eerily quiet as he asked, 'Why? What's in there?'

'It was the main lab. Years ago, when this place was first set up. It was sealed off. For good.'

'Why? What happened?' Catherine asked.

'It was in the 1950s. Before my time, but of course I was briefed when I took the assignment here.'

'Just tell us,' the Doctor snapped.

'There was an accident. Containment leak.'

'Biological?' Brodsky asked, his voice husky.

Klebanov nodded. 'They sealed it solid. Standard procedure.'

'What leaked?' the Doctor asked.

'What about the people?' Catherine said before Klebanov could answer. 'What happened to them?'

Klebanov's face was drained of colour. 'They're still in there.'

The Doctor put his hand on the scientist's shoulder, turned the man to face him. 'I said, what leaked?'

'Does it matter?'

'Of course it matters.'

'He wants to know,' Jack said, 'if it's still dangerous. Because if not – that's the best place to defend. To survive. It's already sealed solid, if we can just get into it.'

'We can blow the wall here,' Levin said, pointing to one of the blocked-off storerooms. 'Yes?'

'Yes, sir,' Krylek told him. 'Probably. Depends how thick it is.'

'You're crazy,' Klebanov said. 'We could all die the moment you open that chamber.'

'Yeah,' Rose told him, 'the alternative being what exactly?'

'Die trying to survive,' the Doctor said. 'Or just die. We need to draw the remotes in so I can get to the ship. Way's blocked at the moment. So, any other offers?'

Whatever the answer was, it was drowned out by the shouts from outside. Several soldiers ran in, and one of them hurried over to Levin and talked to him quietly.

As they spoke, Minin opened a drawer of his desk. He glanced up to see if anyone was watching him and caught Jack's eye. The man hesitated, then pulled a bottle of colourless liquid from the drawer. He pushed it into his jacket pocket.

'We're out of time for debate,' the colonel announced when he had heard the report. 'Lieutenant, get the explosives and gather the men. Bring the civilians. Let's blow that wall and find out whether this thing's still dangerous or not.' He was looking at the Doctor. 'Agreed?'

'What are you waiting for?' the Doctor asked.

There were two storerooms that used to open into the sealed-off main lab. They headed for the one nearest the conference room.

Even so, it was a nightmare journey. The outer wall was crumbling – tentacles reaching through the concrete and thrashing along the corridor. One of the creatures was blocking the end of the corridor that led back towards the main doors. It scraped and squelched against the walls as it dragged itself along.

Krylek and one of the soldiers rolled grenades down the corridor. Everyone ran the other way, and soon the corridor was filled with noise and smoke and confusion.

Brodsky, pale-faced, was keeping pace with Rose when he suddenly disappeared with a cry. She turned round –

to see the man struggling and clawing at the floor of the corridor as he was dragged back. He was looking right at her when his face collapsed in on itself.

Catherine screamed, clutching Rose's arm, and they ran on. In front of them Rose could see Jack pulling Valeria along, urging her onwards. Dust and grit showered from the ceiling. A tentacle fell through in front of them and Rose pushed Catherine aside, so she narrowly missed it.

'Come on!' the Doctor urged from somewhere ahead of them.

Gunfire and explosions from behind.

There were too many people to fit in the storeroom. They were spilling out into the corridor. The Doctor, Levin and Krylek pushed their way through. Jack, Rose and Valeria were left at the back.

The young-old girl just stood, staring into space. Her wrinkled face was stained black from the fire and one side of it had been scalded on the hot metal of the digger's front scoop. Rose smiled at her, but as ever there was no response, no flicker of interest or acknowledgement in the eyes.

Further along the line of people in the corridor, Jack could see the girl's father watching. His expression was as blank and unreadable as his daughter's.

The sound of gunfire echoed along the corridor. Two soldiers appeared round the corner, half running, half stumbling as they turned to fire at the enemy behind them.

But as the first tentacles lashed out after the soldiers, the corridor filled with even more people. They were coming out of the storeroom and back into the corridor. Levin and the Doctor were ushering them out urgently.

'Can't we get through?' Rose wanted to know. 'We can't stay here.'

One of the soldiers cried out as a tentacle wrapped round his leg and brought him down. The end of the corridor was lit with a blue glow as the creature approached.

'They're blowing the wall,' Jack told her. 'You don't want people standing beside it when you set off the charges.'

'If it's a choice…' Rose started to say. But she was interrupted by the arrival of the Doctor.

'Krylek's setting the charges,' the Doctor said. 'But it'll take him a minute.'

'We don't have a minute,' Rose replied.

The creature filled the corridor now – pulsing forwards, tendril-like tentacles whipping and flailing. People pressed back against the cold concrete walls as they tried desperately to keep out of the way.

'Hold it back,' the Doctor said. 'I'll help Krylek. Half a minute. Can you do that?'

'Yes,' Jack said. 'We'll do it.'

'I don't know how,' Rose told him, but the Doctor was already gone.

'I do,' a voice said quietly beside them. It was Minin. He was holding the bottle that he had taken from his desk. He pulled out the stopper and pushed his handkerchief into the bottle.

'You need something to burn. Something more than just the alcohol – that won't be enough. Let me help,' Jack told him.

'I don't need help.' He had a lighter. Was walking slowly along the corridor towards the grotesque creature squeezing its way towards them. 'You get them to safety, Captain. They're my people. I've looked after them as best I can. Now it's your turn. Don't let me down.'

The white of the handkerchief became orange and red as the lighter touched it.

The creature's squeal of triumph was Minin's scream of pain and defiance as it caught him, dragged him towards it. His hand was shaking, ageing, withering. But somehow he managed to smash the bottle to the ground beneath him as he collapsed. Into the flames.

Tentacles dragged him back – through the pool of fire. His clothes were igniting and burning. The creatures were squealing and retreating as the man staggered and stumbled after it – driving it back down the corridor.

Then the corridor was full of dust and smoke. Jack's ears rang with the rumbling roar of the explosion as Krylek's charges ripped through the concrete wall at the back of the storeroom.

'Come on!' The Doctor's voice cut through the confusion. 'Everyone inside, quick!'

Jack grabbed Valeria's hand and led her through to the storeroom. The Doctor was standing just inside the door, ready to slam it shut as soon as everyone was inside. He saw the shock on Rose's face.

'Minin?'

'Bought us some time,' Jack said.

The Doctor nodded. He closed the door. 'Right, everyone wait here while we go inside first. Never know what we might find.'

'What do you expect?' Jack asked.

'Will it be dangerous?' Rose said.

'If the toxin's still active, we're already dead,' Jack told her.

'It isn't,' the Doctor said.

'Sure?'

'Yep. You can tell from the plans that the air conditioning's still connected to this area. Always has been. There was never any toxin. Never any leak.'

'Then why's it sealed?' Jack wondered.

'Let's find out.'

Levin, Krylek and most of the soldiers had already gone through the ragged hole in the end wall. They were standing in a short section of corridor the other side. The floor was coated with a thin layer of dust, but otherwise in the light from the storeroom it looked like every other corridor in the building. At the end of the corridor was a heavy metal door.

'Do we open it?' Levin asked the Doctor.

He nodded. 'Yep.'

'You know what's inside, don't you?' Levin said as Krylek turned to the door.

'Yep.'

The door swung open. Beyond it – blackness.

'Power should be on. There's a light switch on the wall

to your left,' the Doctor called to Krylek. 'It's marked on the plans.'

Fluorescent lights flickered into life as the Doctor followed Krylek and Levin into the huge room. Rose followed, with Jack leading Valeria after them. The rest of the soldiers and the villagers streamed in behind them.

'Close and bar the door,' Levin called out. He did not turn. Like everyone else, he seemed unable to take his eyes off the scene revealed in the room.

It was a huge laboratory. Equipment was piled up on workbenches and antiquated computer systems stood against the walls – tapes and switches and dials and meters. Dust lay heavily over everything so that the glass jars and tubes and pipes seemed opaque. Several surgical trolleys were in the middle of the room, linked up to an arrangement of tubes and pumps, similar to the equipment at Sofia Barinska's house.

But none of this was what held the attention of the people standing inside the door. Fifty people – men, women, children, soldiers, time travellers. All staring at the figures that lay on the trolleys, or sat propped on lab stools so that they leaned over the workbenches. Several were slumped against the walls or computer banks.

All wearing hooded lab coats that had once been white but were now grey with dust and mould. Skeletal arms and bony hands poked out of the ends of the sleeves – pale and brittle as stone. The faces were shrunken, withered husks – mummified and skull-like. Fleshless and grey.

Silence.

Then the creaking, like a ship starting to set sail. Movement. Skull-heads turning slowly towards the doorway. Figures jerking into unsteady life – twisting, rising, shambling...

'Who are they?' Rose breathed.

'The scientists who found the spaceship about fifty years ago,' the Doctor said. 'The scientists who adapted its systems to keep them alive. If you can call this life.'

'It isn't always like this,' said a voice behind them.

Klebanov pushed his way through the crowd of people. He stood staring at the decaying figures that were slowly shuffling towards them.

'He's right. Sofia wasn't like that,' Rose said. 'Not all the time.'

'Takes a lot of energy, though. This lot are waiting for the power to build enough to give them all a dose. Isn't that right?' He was talking to the nearest of the skeletal figures.

Its reply was cracked and dry, like old bones. 'Is it time?' the figure whispered hoarsely. 'Have you found a way for us all to live again? To live for ever?'

But it wasn't talking to the Doctor. It was talking to Klebanov.

The chief scientist nodded. 'It is time. And look...' He turned towards the people crowded into the back of the room, opened his arms to include them all. 'I've brought you food,' he said.

FOURTEEN

From the storeroom behind them came the sound of crashing masonry as the creatures started to force their way through.

'Not doing that great,' Jack said. 'Plan D?'

But the Doctor ignored him. He was talking to Klebanov. 'So was Barinska working with you? Or was she freelance? Cos she'd been here for a while, hadn't she?'

As Klebanov started to reply, the Doctor glanced at Jack. A look, no more – but Jack knew what it meant. Plan D was up to him while the Doctor kept talking.

'She found the ship almost a century ago. Didn't understand it, or what it did for her when she meddled,' Klebanov said.

The Doctor nodded. 'She'd been able to draw off some energy, influenced by the pilot's lingering soul and spirit. But it needed a scientist to adapt it further.'

'Barinska showed me the ship when I took over as director here in 1947.'

'No wonder Minin couldn't find a record of your assignment. He was looking thirty years too late.'

The husks of the scientists were shuffling forwards, arranging themselves in a semicircle around the people. The villagers were frightened but quiet. Everyone watched the Doctor and Klebanov, which gave Jack a chance to tap Lieutenant Krylek on the shoulder. The two of them slipped away, hiding within the group.

'And you all think you're gonna live for ever, is that it? No idea why, of course. That's the pilot's influence again. Wanting you to want to stay alive until you've done his job. So what was the deal? She stays young. Her and you. And the rest of your mates wait here while you sort out a solution, a way of keeping you all young and vibrant?'

'Something like that.'

'Because there isn't enough power for you all, is there? Not while the ship's just ticking over. It only needs one of you, after all. And a lot of the energy it had left wasn't the right sort of power anyway. So it got you to adapt it, play with it – before you all got too old and had to take it easy in here. You tried using the monkeys.' The Doctor gave a short laugh. 'Not such a success, was it, though?'

Klebanov frowned. 'How do you know about that?'

'About what? About how some of your chums got monkeyfied. Give them the energy of a simian and they turn into proto-baboons. And there aren't many bananas to be had out here.'

Klebanov gave a snarl of rage and the other scientists took a step forwards, hands raised now – ready to strike.

'So you had to keep draining human energy. Not too much, though. Don't want people getting too suspicious, and you don't want to run out of food either. So just now and then – the odd sacrifice on the stones, was it? Set the controls in the ship and strap some poor young human down. Get Barinska to blame it on the mythical Vourdulak. That's what happened to Valeria's friend.'

At the edge of the group, Jack froze, listening intently to the Doctor's words. He could see Valeria standing impassively beside Rose.

'He got drained to feed you lot. To keep you going. Top you up like a mobile phone. And then you started on Valeria, only the ship got distracted part of the way through. Switched off when someone answered its little message. Whatever else he may have done, Jack saved her life.'

Jack swallowed. Had he saved her? For this? And was it worth it? He couldn't even begin to think about that, though he knew what the girl's father would say. He nudged Krylek and they edged out of the group towards the side of the room. Towards where Jack calculated the main corridor ran right outside the wall...

The lights flickered. When they came back on they seemed dimmer than before.

'It's started,' the Doctor said. 'As the ship powers up, it'll reverse your modifications. Those remote collectors out there will be after any energy source soon. Not just humans, though they might have acquired a taste for them. One of them's found the power lines, or the generator. It doesn't need to keep you lot alive any more. It thinks help's almost here and it's after all the power it can find for itself.'

'That doesn't matter,' Klebanov said. 'As you said, the problem is one of quantity as much as quality. We can absorb a proportion of the energy. If there is enough, it won't matter where it comes from. And believe me, we have planned for this moment. We have an energy source ready and waiting that will power up the ship and fill us with life for ever. The stronger the ship gets, the stronger we become.'

'What power source?' Rose said. 'Anyway, whatever it is, it won't work if we destroy your dentist's chairs.'

Krylek was the expert. Jack let him get on with positioning the charges against the wall while he stood in front, shielding the soldier – he hoped – from the view of the scientists. One of the emaciated husks turned towards them. Jack made a show of cowering away in apparent fright and horror. The scientist snarled and turned back towards the main group of villagers.

Klebanov was tiring of the conversation with the Doctor. He dismissed Rose's comment with a wave of his hand. 'Not necessary. Oh, Sofia liked to connect herself up in the old-fashioned way, to feel the energy flowing into and through her. She didn't trust our methods.'

Jack could see Vahlen and a few of the others watching him and Krylek, glancing furtively so as not to give anything away, but wondering what they were up to. He nodded, as small a movement as he could so they could understand that they needed to be ready, even if they didn't know what for. At the front of the group, Colonel Levin seemed to pay them no attention at all. But he clasped his hands behind his back – one of them in an obvious thumbs-up.

'Your methods?' the Doctor prompted.

'Direct connection to the ship's storage cells. The energy comes to us as soon as it is available. We can draw it off at will. Once there is enough energy available, we can take what we need to live for a thousand years or more.'

'Wireless network.' The Doctor sounded grudgingly impressed. 'You adapted an energy transmitter from the ship, I s'pose. Neat solution. Bit like how poor old Georgi communicated. I assume you waited till he was in his trance, then gave him different instructions. Won't help, though, cos you'll all be dead soon.'

'And why is that?'

'Because I have to shut down the ship. And once it's gone, you'll find that time catches up with you.'

'I don't think so.'

'I know so.'

Klebanov shook his head. 'But you, Doctor, are never going to leave this room.' He snapped his fingers and at once the other scientists lunged forwards.

At the same moment, there was a crash from behind

and the door vibrated under a sudden impact.

'Those things out there will kill you too!' Rose shouted.

'They won't harm us,' Klebanov said. 'They know that if they drain energy from us it will just feed right back. They'd be wasting their time.'

'They might still try,' the Doctor told him. 'Could be rather painful, I'd think.'

The desiccated remains of the scientists hesitated, turning to look at Klebanov. He frowned. Maybe he hadn't thought of that, Jack realised. Or maybe he was dealing with one problem at a time. Whatever the case, now seemed like the best moment to make their escape.

'Now!' Jack hissed to Krylek.

The lieutenant nodded. 'Just about done,' he murmured. He was holding a small radio-detonator. 'We'd better take cover and hope this works.'

Jack glanced quickly round the room. One of the scientists was heading their way, bony fingers clicking as it stretched out its arms for them. Jack swallowed. 'Er, cover?' The lights were flickering again now – each time they came back less brightly than before.

'What you gonna do – feed us to them?' Rose was shouting above the hammering of the creatures outside. The door was beginning to give way.

'Exactly right,' Klebanov shouted back. He was smiling. 'It should begin to sate their appetite while we slip away to attend to some unfinished business down at the docks. There is a way out of here, you know. But you'll never find it.'

'Don't need to,' the Doctor snapped back. 'Jack!'

'OK,' Jack decided. 'Forget cover. Just do it.' He threw himself to the floor.

The door collapsed inwards and a mass of writhing tentacles stabbed into the room.

The skeletal remains of the scientists hissed in anger and anticipation, and charged forwards ready to drive the villagers – and the Doctor and Rose – back towards the creature forcing its way through the door.

The lights went out.

Then Krylek set off the charge.

Lightning crashed across the darkened room and debris rained down on top of Jack. He coughed and flinched. A flash illuminating clutching hands, frightened faces, the soldiers hustling the villagers towards the smoking gap in the wall.

Jack was on his feet again. Krylek was stumbling beside him, one side of the man's face slick with blood as the lights flickered one last time, then died.

The room was bathed in the eerie, faint glow of the creature that finally heaved itself through the doorway. Plaster and concrete were now crashing down from the ceiling above it.

Shots rang out as the soldiers tried to delay the husk-like scientists charging after the villagers. The emaciated figures staggered back but did not fall.

'Move – move!' Levin was shouting.

The Doctor bundled Rose ahead of him, urging others towards the hole in the wall. Jack, through the gap now, was pulling people through after him as quickly as possible, hoping they didn't jam up the hole in their frightened hurry.

One of the men fell, immediately in danger of being trampled. Jack reached into the mass of crushing bodies and hauled him to his feet, dragging him through – away from the mayhem and out into the corridor.

The man gasped his thanks, wiping a trickle of blood from his face with the trembling back of his hand. His eyes locked for a moment with Jack's – and Jack saw that it was Mamentov. Valeria's father.

Valeria.

He was back at the hole in the wall, trying desperately to see where she was. And glimpsed between the rushing, desperate people, he could see the silhouetted figure of the girl – standing still and alone.

'Rose!' Jack shouted 'Help Valeria!' There was no possibility that he could force his way back inside, and if he waited until everyone else was through it would be too late.

On the other side of the broken wall, Rose nodded. She turned and ran back towards Valeria, struggling against the current of people. Then the wall was a mass of dark bodies, heaving through, and they were lost to sight.

The Doctor was pulling Jack away. 'Go with Levin – keep Klebanov and his mates busy.'

'Why?'

'Weren't you listening? They've got a plan to create a sudden, massive release of energy that will power up the ship and make them all but immortal.'

'Bad, huh?'

'The ship'll be too powerful to stop then. And how would you generate that much energy in a place like this with just a makeshift village, a ruined scientific base and a few old nuclear submarines loaded with barely decommissioned missiles?'

Jack bit his lip as he considered. He didn't need to consider for long. 'Good point. I'm on it. Colonel Levin!' he shouted.

Some of the soldiers had torches. Their beams criss-crossed the bare concrete walls and floor and ceiling of the corridor as they hustled the villagers along.

The Doctor was running with Jack. 'I'll take the villagers.'

'Great – where?'

'You sort out the zombies, I'll defeat the blobs.'

'Deal,' Jack shouted back. 'Where's Rose?'

A line of Levin's men was firing at Klebanov and the scientists, driving them back with a wall of bullets. More of the soldiers were shoving villagers towards the ragged hole in the wall. They poured through, desperately trying to evade the thrashing tentacles of the first of the creatures as it slithered into the large room. Behind it another filled the doorway. The whole room was lit with pale, pulsing blue.

Rose struggled through the mass of people, trying to get back to where Valeria still stood in the middle of the room. A tentacle whipped past the impassive girl, withdrew, lashed out again – this time latching on to one of the men from the village and dragging him back. Rose forced herself not to watch, struggled onwards.

But she knew she wasn't going to get there.

The soldiers were retreating, in an orderly line, despite the advancing creatures. Halfway to the wall, they stopped shooting, turned and ran.

Leaving Valeria alone with Klebanov and his men, and the creatures.

One of the soldiers grabbed Rose as he ran past, dragging her with him towards the way out – away from Valeria.

She shook herself free. But there was nothing she could do.

Klebanov reached out and stroked the girl's wrinkled cheek. 'Have they left you behind?' he said.

She did not move or answer.

The villagers were stumbling and running back down the hill they had so recently climbed. The fire was all but burned out now. The creatures that had been there were gone – having taken a different route to the institute or been burned in the flames.

The Doctor was at the front, encouraging them along. Telling them his plan.

'They'll come after us,' he shouted. 'They'll take any energy they can get, but they still like humans best. Yum yum. So we lead them to where we want them, right?'

'Right,' Vahlen agreed. 'But where is that?'

'Anyone who wants can go home. Or at least to a home at the edge of the village, as far away as possible from the harbour. Cos that's where we're going. We lead the blobbies there, OK?'

'And then what?' Catherine Kornilova asked, breathless and afraid. Her lab coat was stained and torn.

'Must be plenty of fuel left. Even if we have to siphon it out of the subs, though I don't fancy that – tastes disgusting. We get them all there and light up.'

'The dry dock,' Vahlen said. 'That's where most of the fuel is. What's left of it.'

'Great. Let's get set up, lead the blobs to us, and then you can light the blue touch-paper while I nip off and sort out their ship.'

'Simple as that?' Catherine asked.

The Doctor grinned. 'Doubt it.'

Jack and Colonel Levin stood side by side. They were moving back slowly along the corridor, together with the rest of the soldiers. It was a classic retreat. The back row of troops fired, then moved to the front, while the next row fired before moving on itself.

The grotesque figures stumbling after them were being torn to shreds. But still they kept coming – nothing seemed to stop them. The best they could hope for, Jack knew, was to slow the advance. To keep them busy so they didn't realise what the Doctor was up to. At least, for the moment.

Klebanov himself was at the front of the group. His

coat was riddled with bullet holes and his face was cratered and torn. But still he and the others kept coming.

They backed round a sharp corner in the corridor, close to the main entrance now.

And behind them, a creature appeared – tentacles extended as if to welcome them.

'Back!' Levin shouted.

Jack expected – like the others – to find Klebanov and his men waiting. Instead there was another of the creatures.

'They've gone,' Jack realised. 'They knew another way out. They've got away – and left us trapped.'

The soldier next to Jack screamed as a tentacle wrapped round his leg and ripped him off his feet. The whole corridor was now pulsing with blue light as the creatures advanced.

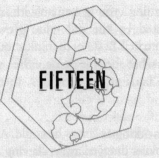

FIFTEEN

Most of the walking dead had gone after Jack and the soldiers. But two of the zombified scientists waited long enough to lead Valeria after them. The girl was still sleepwalking her way through things. Rose pressed back into the shadows, trying not to think what would happen if she ended up trapped between the scientists and the creatures that were pulsing gently but menacingly in the corner of the room.

'She's no good to us. Just a husk, a shell,' one of the scientists told the other. His voice was cracked and brittle, a hoarse whisper. 'No life left. Nothing worth taking. We should throw her to *them*.' He gestured at the creatures across the room.

'They won't want her either,' the other scientist said. 'But she may be useful as a hostage. The villagers protected her before, and while they have hardly hampered us so far, we might need to hold them off.'

They led Valeria through the broken wall. It was a bizarre sight, Rose thought – two zombies from *Dawn of the Dead* escorting a young woman with an aged face, and all illuminated by the pale-blue glow of the blob monsters from hell. Best not to think about it. Best not to think about what she was doing either, she decided, as she glanced back at the creatures, then tiptoed after Valeria.

Krylek was working as fast as he could. Another scream – another soldier dragged away, clawing at the concrete floor as the life and vitality was sapped from him. There were only a few of Levin's troops left now – perhaps a dozen in all.

'Soon would be good,' Jack murmured.

Levin glared at him.

Krylek stepped back from the wall. 'Ready.'

'Do it,' Levin snapped. 'Cover!' he shouted to the survivors.

Tentacles flailed and thrashed as the creatures pressed forwards. Then Krylek pressed the detonator and the world was filled with noise and smoke.

They didn't wait for it to clear, didn't wait to see whether the explosives had blown a hole in the wall. They just threw themselves at it. Smoke clawed at the back of Jack's throat and stung his eyes. But then it cleared and he was coughing and rolling in the cold snow, and laughing and leaping to his feet, and helping Krylek and Levin and the others. And running.

'Where to?' Levin asked.

'After the Doctor. He might need help.'

'*We* might need help,' Krylek said. 'Look!'

From round the end of the low, grey building came the scientists. Klebanov was in the lead. He paused, staring at the soldiers. He might have been surprised, but there was not enough of his face left for any expression. Suddenly he was running, the other scientists stumbling and staggering after him on stick-thin, bony legs.

'Move it!' Levin ordered.

Behind them, when Jack looked over his shoulder, Klebanov was standing watching them run. The other scientists were grouped round him. It seemed to Jack that they were all laughing.

'They won't pose much of a problem,' Klebanov said. It sounded as if he was chewing gravel.

'They're making towards the harbour,' one of the other scientists pointed out.

'Doesn't matter,' Klebanov told him. 'They can't stop us. And when we launch the missiles, the ship will absorb enough power to regenerate us all. Enough power to make us invincible. Enough power to keep us alive for centuries.'

Behind them, in the shadows of the building, pressed close to the wall, Rose watched and listened. Valeria was at the back of the group – perhaps they would just leave her. Forget her. Abandon her.

'What about the girl?' one of the scientists who had brought her asked.

Klebanov walked over to Valeria. He reached out and stroked her cheek. 'She is no use to us,' he said. 'Except... Yes, bring her.'

'Why bother?' one of the others asked. 'She'll just slow us down.'

'Don't be so impatient. That Intelligence captain, he'll be in charge now. And he cares for her. That makes her useful. Gives her a purpose.' Klebanov laughed. 'The only purpose she can have now.'

Some of the villagers had slipped away, escaping into the night. The light flickered on the dark, rusting bodies of the submarines and glinted on the ice-covered water.

The lights were all out now, so Vahlen and some of the others had organised torches – burning lengths of wood scavenged from the dockside and soaked in petrol from a drum outside the inn. The procession of villagers, with the Doctor at the head, made its way through the abandoned harbour and down towards the dry dock at the end.

On the hillside behind them was another procession – a line of pale glowing blue that was following them to the harbour.

'I think they can sense us,' one of the men said. 'Just like old Georgi could sense things without seeing them.'

'I certainly hope so,' the Doctor countered. 'We need those things to believe they've got us where they want us.'

'The dry dock?'

'If that's where the fuel is. We'll check it out, set it up and then I'll leave you to it.'

'What?' Vahlen said. 'You're just going to let us fend for ourselves?'

'You'll do all right. Really.'

'You sound like poor Georgi. So where will you be?'

'Me?' He shrugged. 'Thought I might go for a swim.'

The dry dock was not dry any more. The gates that had once held back the icy sea were buckled and broken and the whole dock was flooded and frozen. Two submarines jutted up from the white landscape – one almost on its side, resting on the other. The hull had rusted through, huge ragged holes of even deeper blackness. The dark shapes towered above the Doctor and the villagers.

'So where's the fuel?' the Doctor asked.

Vahlen led them to the end of the walkway round the dock wall. Another shape loomed up out of the night – black against the white of the ice. It didn't look like fuel drums, more like one of the shapeless creatures asleep and waiting. But Vahlen and several of the men pulled back the tarpaulin that covered the drums of fuel to reveal them piled into a rough, flat-topped pyramid.

'Now what?'

The Doctor blew out a long misty breath. 'Now we cover the ground for as far as we can. We wait for the creatures.'

'And when they're on the oil, we set fire to it,' Vahlen realised.

'Yeah, well. Cross your fingers first and hope you get 'em.'

'And in the meantime you're going swimming?'

He grinned. 'Thought I might. Could walk, but it's a long way from here. Good bracing swim, just the job.'

'You're serious, aren't you?' Vahlen realised.

'Oh yeah.'

'But – you can't go swimming in *this*,' the old man said. He gestured out across the frozen harbour. The wind was whipping up, scattering the flames from the torches and sending sparks flying from the burning wood.

'Well,' the Doctor said, 'I'll have to break the ice first, I suppose.'

The surviving soldiers made their way rapidly down the path to the docks. Jack and Levin led the way. Neither of them was in the mood for much conversation; both of them were agreed that they should find and help the Doctor rather than risk their lives against the scientists.

Further up the hill, a long line of the glowing creatures was making its way after them. Klebanov and his scientists had disappeared into the night, but Jack was pretty sure they too would be making for the docks. He just wanted to get there first.

Their boots crunched on the recent snow. By the time they reached the inn at the edge of the docks, the snow was gone – swept away by the creatures' earlier advance. They headed for the dry dock, where they could see the distant glimmer of firelight. And always the blue glow kept pace behind them, only minutes away.

Jack's foot slipped as they approached the dry dock. He stumbled and almost fell. Beside him, Levin was also having problems.

'Oil,' Lieutenant Krylek said. 'They've spread fuel oil all across here.'

Jack managed to regain his balance. He could see now that the ground was dark and slick. 'What a life,' he grumbled. 'Attacked by the walking dead, chased by life-sucking blobs and now our own team's trying to make me break my neck.' He shook his head and yelled, 'Hey, we're on your side, you know!'

There was an answering shout from up ahead. Two of the men from the village were wheeling a drum of fuel oil along the quay towards them. The barrel was unstoppered so that oil slopped out as it rolled. One of the men, Jack realised, was Mamentov – Valeria's father. As they passed, the man met his gaze and then looked away.

'The Doctor down that way?' Jack asked.

'No,' the second man replied. 'He went for a swim.'

'He what?' Levin said.

Jack just smiled. 'Typical. Come on, then, let's help with these barrels.'

The scientists seemed oblivious to the creatures slithering down the hill with them. But Rose was only too aware that they would kill her as soon as they caught her. She just hoped they didn't realise that there was food following the scientists and Valeria down from the cliffs to the harbour. She concentrated on not making any noise, on keeping to the darkest shadows, on watching where the group in front of her was going.

She knew they were heading for the docks, she just didn't know exactly where. In the distance Rose could see the faint flickering of small fires – the villagers, Jack and the Doctor. Was Klebanov leading them to attack the villagers? Evidently not, as they headed for a different area of the docks. They were close – close enough to make out the people working, rolling drums along the wall surrounding the dry dock and out on to the approach road. But there was an expanse of frozen water between them and the snub-nosed bulk of one of the submarines.

Getting as close as she dared, Rose took shelter behind a pile of rotting crates. Thick ropes coiled like enormous decaying snakes on the top. She peered out at the scientists climbing up to the top of the submarine's conning tower. She could see Valeria with them still, being helped up the ladder. One by one the dark figures disappeared inside the sub, leaving Rose alone outside in the cold.

Perhaps the best thing would be to get to the dry dock and tell the Doctor where Klebanov had gone, which submarine he was on and what he was planning. But while it wasn't far across the frozen harbour, Rose wasn't going to risk falling through into the icy water. And it would take a long time to get there using the access roads. Klebanov would think they were safe and unseen. With luck they would leave Valeria alone and unguarded – confident that she wasn't going to wander off or escape.

Before she knew it, Rose was climbing the ladder after them. The rusting metal flaked away under her hands. It was cold and rough. She hauled herself on to the top of the submarine. Across the harbour she could see the first of the creatures approaching the road to the dry dock, tracking down the villagers and the soldiers. She could make out the small, dark figures hurrying back and forth, desperately spreading as much oil as they could before the creatures arrived. All except one.

That one, she was sure, was Jack – the way he was standing, the way he had his hands in his pockets and appeared to be out sightseeing rather than waiting to fight for his life. Typical. She couldn't see the Doctor anywhere. Also typical.

The circular hatch open at Rose's feet was smaller than she had expected. Another ladder led down into the blackness. 'Well, at least I can just climb out again if things get nasty,' she muttered to herself, and started the climb down.

She was only just inside, her head barely below the level of the roof, when there was a loud clunk from immediately above her. Like the sound of something hitting the hull. Or a long-neglected mechanism shocked into sudden life.

Then a grinding, and what little light there was slowly dimmed and vanished. As the hatch swung shut above her, trapping Rose in the dark with the monsters.

'Did you see that?'

'What?' Jack asked.

'Looked like Klebanov and his old cronies,' Levin said. 'Disappearing into that submarine over there.' He pointed across the small bay to one of the larger subs.

'Nuclear?' Jack asked.

Levin just nodded.

'Don't worry,' a voice said. 'They can't do much harm in there.' It was Vahlen.

'You sure?' Jack asked him.

'The nuclear ones they *did* decommission,' he said. 'Just last year they made the missiles safe in that one. The *St Petersburg*. I remember when it arrived here.'

'Yeah, well, something else is about to arrive, but thanks for the info,' Jack told him. 'Here they come!'

The glowing line of blue was getting ever closer. It looked as if most of the creatures were now on the oil-slick roadway.

'Another minute, then we light her up and hope for the best.'

'Why wait?' someone asked.

'To be sure we get them all.'

'I don't want to get them all.' The someone was the Doctor, and he was standing soaking wet beside Levin and Jack. He struggled into his jacket. 'I need a couple of them to survive.'

'Looks as if you've been having fun,' Jack told him. 'So why's that? And where have you been – the ship?'

'The ship. Long swim, but I wanted a little play with the equipment. That's why you need to light up now and leave a couple of the remotes undamaged.'

Levin shouted orders to his men and the villagers. Those with burning torches stepped towards the dark trail of oil.

'So what do you want a couple of pets for, then?' Jack wondered.

'I want them to chase you.'

'Gee – thanks a million.'

'No problem,' the Doctor said. 'Where's Rose?'

Jack's smile froze. 'She's not with you?'

The Doctor turned a full circle, as if to check. 'She's not with me.'

'Sorry, daft question. She's with Valeria somewhere.'

The torches dipped, in unison, on Levin's orders. Trails of fire leaped from them across and along the roadway. Orange and red raced towards the harbour, and the creatures. They squealed and shuddered and retreated from the flames.

'She can't have been daft enough to follow Klebanov into that sub,' Jack said as they watched.

The flames were leaping high into the air, engulfing the creatures. They thrashed and tried to retreat. But the creatures further back were blocking the way, seemingly unaware of the danger until the flames reached them too. Smoke curled upwards – dark and sinister against the night sky.

'What sub?' the Doctor said as the fire crackled and spat.

Only at the very back of the line did any of the creatures survive. One slithered away rapidly, spilling fire and sparks. Another seemed unscathed, waiting patiently while its fellows melted and burned.

'The *St Petersburg*.' Jack pointed. He had to shield his face from the heat and his eyes were smarting. 'Nuclear job.'

'I told you to keep them away from the missiles.'

'Ah, it's OK. They've all been decommissioned.'

'OK?' The Doctor was aghast. He grabbed Jack's shoulder and turned him to stare into his face. 'OK? Hello – anyone home in that skull of yours? This is volcano day all over again.'

'Oh, wise up, Doctor. The missiles have been decommissioned, so what can he do?'

The Doctor turned away. For a moment Jack thought he was going off to sulk, but he was looking for someone. 'Catherine!' he yelled, and the woman ran over.

'I think we've done it.' She was smiling and excited, relieved. 'There are only a couple that have escaped.'

'As planned,' Jack told her proudly.

'There'll be more that haven't got here yet,' the Doctor snapped. 'Don't get complacent. Now, tell him about the missiles,' the Doctor said more quietly. 'Tell him about the missiles on the *St Petersburg*. Tell him what happened to them.'

'Oh, don't worry about them,' she said, unconsciously echoing Jack's words.

'You see.'

'They were decommissioned last year.' She smiled thinly as Jack grinned at her. 'Klebanov did it himself. Insisted.'

Jack's grin vanished. He turned to stare into the flames. 'Volcano day,' he said.

SIXTEEN

There was light further along. The metal corridor echoed to Rose's every footstep. She could hear the drip-drip-drip of water constantly around her. What light there was bled red through the claustrophobic, pipe-lined tunnel.

She shuffled along as quietly as she could, feet dragging through several inches of icy water. Voices now – low and indistinct – from up ahead. Where the light was coming from.

Rose had her back pressed against the cold wall. Pipework and cables dug into her, even through the thick coat, as she edged along, closer to the voices and the light. At last, she was just outside what she could now see was a control room. Several of the scientists were grouped round a bank of equipment, trying to coax some life back into it. Klebanov stood watching, ordering, impatient.

'We shall need to recommission the missile,' one of the scientists told him. His face was a hollow husk and his eyes were blank, dark sockets. 'The detonator will have to be reset.'

Klebanov nodded. 'Get on with it.'

Rose pressed back still further, closing her eyes tight shut. There was no way that the man – the creature that had been a man – could miss her as he came out of the control room.

Nothing happened. She opened one eye, just a fraction. There was no one there. She leaned forwards far enough to peep into the room again – and now she could see that there was another doorway out of it. That must be the way to the missile bay. And standing beside the door, staring vacantly into space and ignored by everyone, was Valeria.

'And you think your plan will work?' Jack asked.

'Yeah, no problem.' The Doctor nodded vigorously. 'Well, maybe a few problems, but it'll work.'

'A few problems? What about my risking life and limb to tempt one of those things after me?'

The Doctor sighed. 'Well, of course, if you're not interested in saving the human race I can always find someone else. Thought you'd like first dibs.'

'Cos I got us into this mess in the first place?'

'Look, d'you want a debate or d'you want to save the planet?'

Jack shook his head. 'All right, I'm on it. As soon as the fire dies down a bit.'

The road was still burning, but in patches now rather than a mass of unbroken flame. Some of the creatures were still moving weakly. They might recover. They might come slithering on again once the heat was off, Jack thought. The one that was unscathed was pulsing angrily at the end of the roadway, as if waiting for him.

'It's dying down now,' the Doctor said.

'I'll give it another minute.'

The Doctor snorted. 'Wimp!' He squared his shoulders and turned towards the fire, grinning. 'Race you.' And he was off, running.

Jack hesitated, sighed, swore, and ran after him. Levin and Krylek, Catherine and the villagers stared after them in astonishment. Two dark figures running through fire...

The dry, emaciated husks that had once been people crowded round the main control panel on the bridge of the submarine. They seemed to have forgotten all about Valeria. Rose could hear the odd comment and observation as they examined and repaired the controls. They seemed to be preparing the systems for a launch.

'Arming procedure under way.'

The important thing was that they were all busy – all concentrating on the panels in front of them. Leaving Valeria standing alone and unobserved. Rose edged into the room. Slowly, hardly daring to breathe, she tiptoed over to where the girl was standing.

'We'll need to refuel the launch vehicle.'

Valeria looked back at her through rheumy eyes as Rose put her finger to her lips. Bit daft, she thought, as soon as she did it. Not as if the poor girl would even know what she was doing, and she wasn't about to shout out either.

'That can be done automatically from here. Just as we could close the hatch to deter unwanted guests.'

Gently, Rose took the girl's hand and led her slowly, carefully, quietly across the bridge.

'Just as well. We don't want to be in the bay when the rocket goes up.'

The other door was closer, and if she was going to stop them, she needed to get to the launch bay – wherever that was. And she couldn't afford to leave behind a possible hostage. But while Rose was careful to make no noise, it did not matter to Valeria. The girl stumbled along with Rose, her feet splashing in the pools of water on the decking and scraping along the rusty metal.

Mercifully, the scientists were totally absorbed in their work. Rose got to the doorway, pulling Valeria after her.

But the girl's arm caught on the edge of the open hatchway, dragging it with her. A scraping, metallic groan. Rose winced and froze. For a moment none of the scientists seemed to have noticed, just went on working.

Then Klebanov slowly turned to see what the noise was. His eyes locked for an instant with Rose's. His shattered face twisted into a snarl of rage.

'Run!' Rose shouted at Valeria, though she knew at once it would do no good. She dragged the girl through the hatchway after her, then turned back and grabbed the door that had betrayed them.

It was heavy and stiff. Rose heaved with all her might and slowly it began to move – grating, scraping, protesting. Klebanov and several of his colleagues were running towards them – visible through the slowly narrowing gap between door and hatchway.

A hand closed on the door, skeletal fingers wrapped round it as the withered scientist started to drag the door open again.

With a final heave, Rose dragged it shut. A squeal of rusty metal; a crack of dry bone; a clang of door into frame. Something splashed into the shallow water at Rose's feet. She didn't look to see what it was. There were catches round the edge of the hatchway – you could twist them across into a slot in the hatch to seal the door. The first one refused to move.

The second was stiff, but Rose was able to slide it round just enough to keep the door shut. For now.

Already it was shaking as the scientists hammered on the other side and tried to drag it open again. The metal catch was bending, cracking, flaking rust as it split away from the join.

Rose grabbed Valeria's hand again and pulled her down the red-lit corridor.

Jack shivered from the cold while his jacket steamed from the heat of the flames. The fire had all but died away. Some of the creatures were moving hesitantly from side to side, tendrils and tentacles flopping and twitching across the road.

Before leaving him on the quay, the Doctor had told Jack what he wanted, and why he wanted it. It made as much sense and sounded as sensible as any of the Doctor's last-minute schemes. And as usual certain elements were just completely mad. The first and most extreme of these being Jack's mission to get himself chased by one or more of the creatures. The more the better, the Doctor had told him. One was pushing the limit so far as Jack was concerned.

The villagers were soon going to have a problem, Jack could see now. Once the creatures began to recover, once the flames had died away, then the surviving remotes from the ship would be on the move again. Not only that, but while they had been able to see that one of the creatures had escaped injury, Jack could now see several more approaching the docks. Perhaps they had been further away, in the village maybe. Or perhaps the ship was able to generate more of them to replace any that were damaged or injured.

No time to hang around, though. If he stopped to think about it he might realise just how suicidally stupid this whole venture really was. So he thrust his hands into his jacket pockets and walked swiftly along the quay. Whistling.

It seemed at first that the undamaged creature might just ignore him. After all, there was more 'food' waiting back at the dry dock. How close would Jack have to get to convince the thing he was worth chasing? Could he convince it? He stopped whistling and walked slowly towards the pale-blue blob-like creature. It pulsed and quivered as he approached and he was ready at any moment to turn and run.

Still it did not seem interested. If he got much closer he could reach out his arm and touch the thing. Not that he was about to.

Arm. Touch.

He realised almost too late.

Jack leaped back, just as a tentacle slashed through the air in front of him. A tentacle that Jack must have almost stepped on to get this close. 'Clever,' he told the creature. 'But not quite clever enough. Still, dinner's here now – so come and get it.'

He backed away, smiling with grim satisfaction as the creature slithered after him. The smile faded as he turned – and saw two more of the creatures approaching through the harbour.

'Oh… docks!' he said.

The St Petersburg loomed dark and forbidding against the slate grey of the night sky. Mist curled round the conning tower and over the bulbous hull. The Doctor walked the entire length of the submarine and then back again. He noted where the missile tubes were and where the launch bay must therefore be. He made an informed guess about where the bridge must be situated. He spent a moment considering getting inside through the main hatch. He wondered if Rose was inside somewhere, or whether he only needed to worry about the missiles.

Then he sprinted for the deck and knelt down by the secondary hatch, close to the front of the boat. His sonic screwdriver whirred and glowed. Blue against rust-brown as the hatch unlocked and swung open.

There was one creature on either side of the road. They scraped and slithered between two of the rotting submarines, perhaps feeling for any energy that might be lingering in the reactors or batteries. The creature behind Jack was heaving itself after him more rapidly, and he was running to keep ahead of the thrashing tentacles.

Running straight at the other creatures.

It was either run between them or dive off the quay and into the freezing water. He'd tried that before and he wasn't keen to do it again. Was there room to get between the creatures? He would soon find out.

Blue glowing walls either side of him. Tentacles slapping down. The walls closing in. The creature behind him following, squeezing between its fellows. Jamming them apart so they couldn't close in on him any more. Jack ducked as something whipped past his head. He kept running.

And emerged the other side. The creatures seemed to have stuck together. They squelched and squealed as they tried to break free from each other and follow him.

Jack could wait. He sat on the low wall that ran along the side of the roadway and got his breath back. 'Sort yourselves out, will you?' he shouted at the creatures. 'We've got an appointment back at the lab and I don't want to be late. Especially,' he added more quietly, 'if this is going to be my own funeral.'

The whole submarine echoed with the metallic clang of the door from the bridge breaking open.

Rose and Valeria were running. Their feet slapping and splashing and thumping on the deck plates. Rose had to drag the girl – her natural state seemed to be at rest, so anything else needed effort and encouragement.

Ahead of them was another metal hatchway – standing half closed. Rose put her shoulder to it, still running. Her whole body shook and ached from the impact, but the heavy door swung slowly open. Rose was stepping into a large room. It must be the whole width and height of the submarine. A line of blunt-nosed, grey tubes stood on end along one side. They were held in huge metal brackets that were attached to a system of linked chains and belts to move them. Missiles.

And standing by one of the missiles, supervising the attachment of pipes and tubes and examining the open side, were three of the scientists. They turned and stared across at Rose and Valeria.

'Maybe not,' Rose decided. 'Sorry.'

But she could already hear the thump of approaching feet from the corridor behind her. 'Come on!' she shouted at Valeria, hoping that for once the girl might respond. Rose gripped her hand tightly and pulled her into the missile bay, across the room, towards the door on the far side, as fast as she could.

One of the scientists turned back to his work. Another – stick thin, face barely more than a skull and lab coat peppered with bullet holes seeping dark, viscous fluid, started towards them. He half ran, half staggered, as if his legs were unused to working.

Through the door, the scientists clutching at them, almost catching Valeria, hissing with anger.

Rose pushed the heavy door shut, trying to close it against the scientists pushing from the other side. But without success. Slowly the door was being forced open again.

Then a hand closed on Rose's shoulder. She yelped, turned, eyes wide with fear.

'Found you, then,' the Doctor said happily.

'You're not the only one,' she told him. 'Give us a hand.'

He shook his head. 'Nah. I want to talk to Klebanov.'

'But they're going to launch a missile.'

'I know.'

The hatchway door was swinging open again and two of the scientists stood there, watching. Between them, across the missile bay, Rose could see Klebanov and the others arriving.

'What you going to tell them?' Rose said quietly, feeling empty and defeated.

'Only what they should already know. That this missile's going nowhere. And that whatever they might think, they've been dead for years.'

* * *

His foot crunched through something on the concrete floor. Jack glanced down and then swallowed hard. He carefully removed his foot from the dried, withered chest of an emaciated body. His entire world was tinged with blue.

'You guys have a lot to answer for,' he shouted over his shoulder. 'So the Doctor had better be right about this. Can you smell it yet? D'you still need me?'

The first of the creatures was slithering across the threshold and into the corridor. It was glowing brighter now. Maybe it really could sense the power. Maybe it really was heading not for Jack but for a far greater source of energy.

He thought for a moment, then changed direction. Instead of heading for the break in the wall that led into the central laboratory, Jack took a side passage. He waited there and watched as the creatures slithered past, one by one. Three of them so far. Maybe others were on their way – the more the better.

'Tell you what,' Jack said, stepping back into the main corridor and watching the blue glow fade as the creatures turned the corner at the end. 'Tell you what, I'll just leave you guys to it. I've got a girl to find. Couple of girls, in fact. You do your stuff, I'll do mine.'

It was a long journey back down to the docks, but Jack was running all the way.

Colonel Levin and Lieutenant Krylek stood with Catherine Kornilova. The villagers were gathered behind them, the soldiers fanned out in a defensive formation across the end of the dry dock.

Around them the dark hulks of the submarines hemmed them in. The fires had all but burned out. Black smoke coiled lazily into a charcoal sky, lit blue by the pale glow from the end of the quay.

'Looks like we're on our own this time, sir,' Krylek said.

'Looks like it,' Levin agreed grimly.

'The Doctor has a plan,' Catherine told them. 'He's up to something.'

'Then let's hope it works. And let's hope it works soon.'

The first of the creatures was pushing its way through the drifting smoke. The heat from the fire was making its glowing skin hiss and spit, but still it came.

'Grenades?' Levin asked.

'None left, sir,' Krylek told him.

'Ammunition?'

'Pretty low, sir. For what it's worth.'

'Ideas?'

'There's a life belt over there,' Catherine said.

Both soldiers turned to stare at her. To their surprise she was smiling. 'I can tell you're not local. And you're army not navy.'

'The water is iced over,' Levin pointed out. 'And if it weren't, one life belt would hardly help us all. And if it did we'd freeze to death.'

'Retreat, sir?' Krylek suggested.

'I don't think there's anywhere very much to go. A bit of beach, then cliffs. We might as well stay here.'

They watched as Catherine ran over to a wooden box attached to the railings round the top of the wall surrounding the dock. The hinges were rusted solid, but the wood was old and rotten so she ripped away the front. Levin could see the pale shape of the life belt inside the box – what was she up to? She grabbed something and came running back. It wasn't the life belt.

'Here,' Catherine said, breathless. 'You know what to do with this better than me, I expect.' She handed something to Levin.

A flare pistol and three cartridges.

He nodded, impressed. 'It won't hold them back for long,' he warned. 'But it'll give them something to think about.'

'Refuelling 70 per cent complete,' the scientist watching the gauge said.

Klebanov had a pistol and he was pointing it squarely at the Doctor. Rose was pleased he didn't point it at her, but miffed that he obviously didn't think she was a threat. Most of all, though, she was worried he might shoot the Doctor.

'Tell him,' Rose said.

'Tell me what?' Klebanov sounded amused. Maybe he was smiling – it was no longer possible to tell.

'Tell him,' Rose said again.

'Right.' The Doctor nodded, pointing at Klebanov. 'I'm telling you,' he said.

'I'm so scared,' the chief scientist replied.

The others cackled and laughed.

'Now 75 per cent complete,' the scientist by the gauge said as the amusement died down.

'So what's the plan, then, eh?' the Doctor asked. 'Refuel a missile and then launch, is that it? Big bang somewhere up above us, massive airburst energy release. Ship absorbs the energy and powers up fully. But it's not going anywhere, so the energy is all channelled to you lot through the transmitter in your lab. It won't all be useful, but you'll manage to convert enough of it to regenerate yourselves and keep going.'

'That's right,' Klebanov agreed. 'You're very clever, Doctor.'

'We're 80 per cent complete.'

'Oh, I'm a genius. And it doesn't take a genius to work out that a lot of the energy won't be converted and will pretty much flatten this part of the world. We'll be in the eye of the storm here, safe and sound close to the ship as it absorbs the blast. But the radioactive cloud will spread out and maybe get as far as the nearest cities. Kill a few million straight away. A few more million over the next year or two. But what the hell, it won't affect you and your supermen – you'll be laughing.'

'As you say.'

'Except it isn't going to happen.'

'Now 85 per cent complete.'

'I really don't think you or anyone else can stop us,' Klebanov told him.

Rose was beginning to think he was right. The

Doctor was just talking. Valeria wasn't about to do anything – simply standing with them and staring into space. Goodness knows where Jack was or what was happening outside.

'We're 90 per cent complete. Beginning pre-launch checks.'

Which just left Rose. 'In for a penny,' she muttered. The gun was still pointing at the Doctor. All Klebanov's attention was on him. All the other scientists were either busy at the controls or watching the Doctor. Maybe that was it – maybe that was his plan: to distract them so Rose could act.

'Refuelling now 95 per cent complete. Pre-launch checks all positive. Primary ignition in ten seconds.'

She didn't think about it.

'*Nine*.'

Just hurled herself at the controls.

'*Eight*.'

Crashed through the group of scientists.

'*Seven*.'

Slammed into the control panel.

'*Six*.'

And stared. What did she do now? Where was the abort button? Was there an abort button? Or would it be a switch?

'*Five*.'

Behind her someone was yelling at Klebanov not to shoot – not to risk damaging the controls. Maybe she should just thump every button and press every switch and twist every dial.

'Four.'

But it was too late. Hard, cold hands grabbed her arms and shoulders.

'Three.'

Dragged her back from the controls. Turned her away.

'Two.'

Her eyes met the Doctor's.

'One.'

'Sorry,' Rose said.

'Good effort,' the Doctor said quietly.

But his words were almost drowned out by the sound. A warning klaxon blaring out.

The scientist watching the gauges was shaking his head, thumping at the controls. 'Systems failure.' His voice was a hollow rasp. 'Complete shutdown.'

Klebanov stared in disbelief, the remains of his face contorted with rage. The gun was shaking as he struggled to hold it steady. 'What's wrong?' he hissed. 'What happened? The missile was fully fuelled.'

The Doctor stood absolutely still, meeting the man's gaze. 'That gauge just tells you it's full, not what it's full of. I'm not an expert,' he said, 'but this is the sort of thing that happens if someone clever like me disconnects your refuelling hose from the main supply and attaches it instead to the torpedo tubes' seawater intake.'

Any reply was lost in the shouts from the doorway, as Captain Jack exploded into the control room and hurtled towards the scientists holding Valeria.

Klebanov was shaking. He needed both hands to hold the gun. Behind him the other scientists were shaking too. But not with anger. Slowly, they sank to their knees, as if the energy was being drained from them. Only Klebanov stayed upright. His finger tightened on the trigger. Fired.

Just as Jack smashed the gun out of the man's hands and sent it spinning across the room.

'What is happening to us?' Klebanov hissed as he too sank to his knees.

'Your time's up,' the Doctor said. 'It's over.'

'But… how?'

'I led the ship's remotes back to the lab,' Jack said. 'To your transmitter.'

The last of the flares impacted on the glutinous hide of the creature. Levin could see it burrowing its way into the jelly-like mass. A line of fire scorching through the thing – the skin and flesh melting and dripping away. The flare exploded deep within and fire burned its way out again, sending chunks of glowing blue spattering across the roadway.

But behind the stricken creature another was moving forwards, pushing its fellow out of the way as it hungrily slithered towards the people at the end of the dock.

'I guess this is it, then,' Catherine said.

'I guess so.' Levin turned to his men. He cleared his throat. He wasn't sure quite what he was going to say, but he was going to say something – something about honour and privilege and determination and camaraderie and fallen comrades.

But before he could speak, Lieutenant Krylek was grabbing his shoulder and turning him back. 'Look, sir – look!'

The creature at the front of the line had stopped. It seemed to be sinking into the ground – collapsing in on itself. Melting away. Viscous blue liquid was running across the roadway and dripping over into the icy harbour. The glow faded, pulsing more weakly with every second. The other creatures were the same – melting, fading, dying.

'What's happening?' Catherine said quietly.

Levin could only shake his head. 'I've no idea. But let's not complain.'

'The transmitter is the single greatest power source in the area,' the Doctor told them. 'Has to be. All the power the creatures find and send back to the ship, you fixed to channel to that transmitter and out to you.'

'So now the blobs have got it,' Rose realised, 'they can't get their power any more.'

'That's right. More than that, though. It's a loop. The blobs get the power from the transmitter and send it back to the ship.'

Klebanov was trying to speak. But while his jaw was moving, the only sound was a cracked coughing. He was shaking, on his knees, pitching forwards. All around him the others were crumbling to dust – bones disintegrating, bodies collapsing in on themselves.

'Then the ship sends it to the transmitter,' Jack went on. 'And the blobs send it back to the ship.' He was standing with Valeria. The girl's face was wet – water from the leaking pipes, or perspiration.

'And with each loop, each cycle,' the Doctor said, 'a little bit of power gets lost. Because it's all happening incredibly fast, it drains away fairly quickly. Pretty soon, the ship will be safely powered down.'

'What will happen then?' Rose asked, unable to look away as Klebanov pitched forwards onto his face. His hands were dry bone, then powder. His lab coat was stained and torn and empty.

'You're looking at it.'

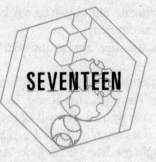

SEVENTEEN

'I was worried about you,' Jack said to her. They were standing in the stone circle.

Levin and Krylek and the soldiers were waiting nearby for the helicopters. Now the radio interference was gone they had called for back-up – there was rebuilding to do and Levin had bullied his superiors into funding it. He had pointed out that Catherine was willing and able to detail the illegal and dangerous work that Klebanov had been carrying out. Even though no one in the Kremlin had any idea what it might be, the implications were enough given that the institute had been set up to research biological weapons and that Levin had given them a rough estimate of the military and civilian death toll.

'I had to come back,' Jack went on. 'To make sure you were all right.'

'I was fine, thanks,' Rose said from behind him.

'You can take care of yourself,' he replied, without turning. He was still facing Valeria, still holding her limp, lifeless hand. 'She doesn't even know I'm here, does she?' he said quietly.

'I shall look after her,' Mamentov said. 'I see now that it is my duty.'

Fedor Vahlen clapped his hand on the man's shoulder. 'I will help you, my friend,' he said. 'It is what Pavel would have wanted. We will all help.'

'Thank you,' Mamentov said. He reached out and took his daughter's hand from Jack. 'And thank you, Captain. You have taught an old man something he should already have known.'

Jack nodded sadly. 'I'm sorry I can't do more.' He looked into Valeria's expressionless, wrinkled face. He stroked her fine blonde hair with the back of his hand. Then he turned away.

'Time we were on our way,' the Doctor said. 'If you're done with the goodbyes.'

Rose nudged Jack with her shoulder. 'Hey,' she said. 'We did good.'

'Did we?'

'Oh yeah,' the Doctor said. 'Would have happened sooner or later. And we defeated the villains. Saved the world.'

Jack nodded. 'But sometimes, you know, that just doesn't seem to be enough.'

'It's a good start,' Rose said.

It was beginning to snow. Large, lazy flakes were twisting down from the sky and settling on the smooth stones of the circle. Jack paused, sighed and turned back towards the little group of villagers who had gathered to see them off. They couldn't know where they were going or how they intended to travel, but they seemed to know that it was goodbye.

The Doctor and Rose stopped too. The Doctor waved. 'Cheerio, then,' he called.

'Come on,' Rose said. 'It's freezing.'

'I'll catch you up.' Jack was running back through the thickening snow. He stopped in front of Valeria and looked again into her glassy, unfocused eyes. 'I forgot to say goodbye.' He leaned forwards and kissed her gently on the cheek.

And slowly, with no change of expression, she reached her arms around Jack and held him tight. Just for a few moments. In the cold, cold snow.

Acknowledgements

As ever, I am indebted to the usual suspects – my editor, Steve Cole, the creative team at the *Doctor Who* production office in Cardiff, especially Helen Raynor and Simon Winstone, who keep us honest, and Russell T Davies, who keeps us enthused and inspired.

One of the main design elements on our *Doctor Who* book covers – and the DVDs and other merchandise – is the distinctive typeface used for the titles. It's a terrific 'distressed' design created by the talented Lloyd Springer and available from the TypeArt Foundry – at www.TypeArt.com. I mention this not just so everyone can rush off and produce nice-looking *Doctor Who*-style lettering, but because the name of the font is Deviant Strain. When I discovered that, I just knew it must be not only the Doctor's own typeface but also one of his adventures. So my thanks to Lloyd and the team for the great design, the inspiring title and their kind permission to use it for this book. I hope I've done them justice.

About the Author

Justin Richards is the Creative Director for the BBC's range of *Doctor Who* books and has written a fair few of them himself. As well as writing for stage, screen and audio, he is also the author of *The Invisible Detective* novels for children. His novel for older children, *The Death Collector*, will be published in 2006.

Justin lives in Warwick, with a lovely view of the famous castle and about as far from the sea – and any submarines – as you can get in Britain.

DOCTOR·WHO

Monsters and Villains

By Justin Richards

ISBN 0 563 48632 5

UK £7.99 US $12.99/$15.99 CDN

For over forty years, the Doctor has battled against the most dangerous monsters and villains in the universe. This book brings together the best – or rather the worst – of his enemies.

Discover why the Daleks were so deadly; how the Yeti invaded London; the secret of the Loch Ness Monster; and how the Cybermen have survived. Learn who the Master was, and – above all – how the Doctor defeated them all.

Whether you read it on or behind the sofa, this book provides a wealth of information about the monsters and villains that have made *Doctor Who* the tremendous success it has been over the years, and the galactic phenomenon that it is today.

DOCTOR · WHO

Only Human
By Gareth Roberts
ISBN 0 563 48639 2
UK £6.99 US $11.99/$14.99 CDN

Somebody's interfering with time. The Doctor, Rose and Captain Jack arrive on modern-day Earth to find the culprit – and discover a Neanderthal Man, twenty-eight thousand years after his race became extinct. Only a trip back to the primeval dawn of humanity can solve the mystery.

Who are the mysterious humans from the distant future now living in that distant past? What hideous monsters are trying to escape from behind the Grey Door? Is Rose going to end up married to a caveman?

Caught between three very different types of human being – past, present and future – the Doctor, Rose and Captain Jack must learn the truth behind the Osterberg experiment before the monstrous Hy-Bractors escape to change humanity's history for ever…

DOCTOR·WHO

The Stealers of Dreams

By Steve Lyons

ISBN 0 563 48638 4

UK £6.99 US $11.99/$14.99 CDN

In the far future, the Doctor, Rose and Captain Jack find a world on which fiction has been outlawed. A world where it's a crime to tell stories, a crime to lie, a crime to hope, and a crime to dream.

But now somebody is challenging the status quo. A pirate TV station urges people to fight back. And the Doctor wants to help – until he sees how easily dreams can turn into nightmares.

With one of his companions stalked by shadows and the other committed to an asylum, the Doctor is forced to admit that fiction can be dangerous after all. Though perhaps it is not as deadly as the truth…